The Inuk Mountie Adventure

Books by Eric Wilson

The Tom and Liz Austen Mysteries

1. Murder on *The Canadian*
2. Vancouver Nightmare
3. The Case of the Golden Boy
4. Disneyland Hostage
5. The Kootenay Kidnapper
6. Vampires of Ottawa
7. Spirit in the Rainforest
8. The Green Gables Detectives
9. Code Red at the Supermall
10. Cold Midnight in Vieux Québec
11. The Ice Diamond Quest
12. The Prairie Dog Conspiracy
13. The St. Andrews Werewolf
14. The Inuk Mountie Adventure

Also available by Eric Wilson

Summer of Discovery
The Unmasking of 'Ksan
Terror in Winnipeg
The Lost Treasure of Casa Loma
The Ghost of Lunenburg Manor

The Inuk Mountie Adventure

A Tom Austen Mystery

by

ERIC WILSON

HarperCollins*Publishers*Ltd

Special thanks to First Air, Sadie Whitemoon, and the students and staff of Duncan Christian School and Quqshuun Ilihakvik Centre, Gjoa Haven.

As in his other mysteries, Eric Wilson writes here about imaginary people in a real landscape.

http://www.harpercollins.com

First published in hardcover by HarperCollins Publishers Ltd: 1995
First published in paperback by HarperCollins Publishers Ltd: 1996

Canadian Cataloguing in Publication Data

Wilson, Eric
    The Inuk mountie adventure

(A Tom Austen mystery)
ISBN 0-00-648197-3

I. Title.   II. Series: Wilson, Eric. A Tom Austen mystery.

PS8595.I583I58 1996   jC813'.54   C95-933332-0
PZ7.W55In 1996

---

96 97 98 99 ❖ OPM 10 9 8 7 6 5 4 3 2 1

Printed and bound in the United States

cover design: Richard Bingham
cover and chapter illustrations: Richard Row
logo photograph: Lawrence McLagan

Dedicated with love to
Flo Connolly,
angel by my side

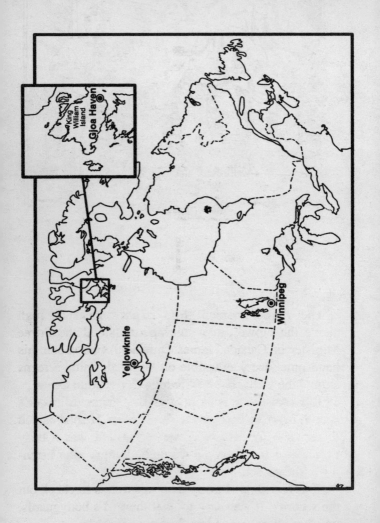

1

"I believe in U-SAC!"

The words boomed from mighty speakers, high above the crowd. At a microphone stood the Prime Minister of Canada, James Dunbar. As he spoke, his handsome face was visible on large television screens around the walls of the Winnipeg Convention Centre.

Tom Austen was watching the Prime Minister's speech from the doorway to the kitchen. He had landed a part-time job as a dishwasher, and it was a busy evening—a lot of people would be hungry after listening to the speech.

Tom had slipped away from his duties to check out the security. It was easy to spot the PM's bodyguards, who had short hair and restless eyes.

Tom's own eyes studied the scene for signs of

trouble. Above the crowd, huge balloons were labelled *Vote YES for U-SAC!* Could the balloons secretly contain a deadly nerve gas, waiting to be spilled on the unsuspecting throngs? No—Tom shook his head at that theory.

But what if one of those TV cameras was a fake and had a gun concealed inside, ready to be fired at the PM? Dunbar would be a sitting duck, centre stage in the glare of spotlights.

"Yes," the Prime Minister cried, "the future prosperity of Canada is guaranteed. Once U-SAC is a reality, our financial problems will be easy to solve. I can assure you . . . "

Tom's eyes continued to sweep the scene. What if an assassin with an assault rifle lurked behind a spotlight? What if . . .

"Hey, kid!"

One of the junior chefs gestured angrily at Tom. "Get back to work! You want to get fired, your first night on the job?"

"I wouldn't mind," Tom murmured. Back at his sink, he plunged his hands into deep water; potato peels and scum floated on the gray surface. "Disgusting," he muttered to himself, beginning to scrub a grease-encrusted pan, "absolutely disgusting."

"Hi."

A dark-eyed little girl, aged about six, stood beside the sink. She was clutching some pretty flowers. "These are for the Prime Minister," she told Tom. "But Mommy says I can't meet him."

The girl's mother smiled. She was rolling pastry at a marble-topped table; like the other workers, she wore an apron over her white uniform. "Rosie adores Prime Minister Dunbar. I can understand why—those blue eyes are amazing. At her school, they showed a movie about his life. Rosie insisted I bring her to work tonight, even though she can't meet the Prime Minister."

Drying his hands, Tom smiled at the girl. "You want to see him, in person?"

Rosie nodded.

Tom glanced around—there was no sign of the junior chef. Taking Rosie's hand, he quickly led her around a corner to the doorway that led to the convention floor. "There he is," Tom said, pointing. Rosie's eyes glowed.

"What's he speeching about?" she asked.

"Pretty soon, Canadians are going to have a special vote."

"Do I get one?"

"No," Tom replied. "Only adults get to vote. There is a referendum being held. People get to vote yes or no to joining Canada and the United States together into a single country."

Rosie waited silently for more information.

"People call the proposed new country U-SAC," Tom explained. "That's short for the official name— The United States of America plus Canada. There'd be a new flag, and no border. The Prime Minister thinks it's a good idea, so he's travelling across the country giving speeches. That's why he's in Winnipeg."

"Are you voting for a new country?"

"I'm only 15," Tom replied, "too young to vote. But I kind of like the country we've got."

The Prime Minister's speech ended, and a brass band began performing a happy song called "The Yellow

Rose of Texas." Cheering and applauding, the crowd pressed toward the Prime Minister, straining to touch his hand. More balloons were released, and they soared up to the ceiling far above; each said *YES!* in large letters.

Leaving the stage, the PM and his bodyguards began moving through the crowd. Dunbar was enormously popular, and everyone was happy to see him. Flash cameras popped constantly in the Prime Minister's face, but he never stopped smiling.

"He's coming our way, Rosie. Maybe you can give him those flowers."

But Rosie's mother beckoned to them. "Tom, come back to the kitchen and bring Rosie. Right now! I'm nervous, with that big crowd. What if there's a stampede?" She glanced back at the kitchen. "If that crabby junior chef finds me gone, I'll be fired. Come this instant, Tom—please!" She hurried away.

Tom smiled, knowing a stampede was unlikely. Taking Rosie by the hand, he began walking along the hallway in the direction of the kitchen.

At that moment, a loud BANG! sounded from the convention floor, followed by screams.

* * *

Startled, Tom looked back. Incredible noise filled the hallway—yells of horror, shouted warnings, hysterical shrieks of terror.

Prime Minister Dunbar was racing down the hallway from the convention floor; behind him came the bodyguards. Seeing the Prime Minister, Rosie ran forward with the flowers.

"Out of my way," the man cried, sweeping the child aside with a big hand.

The Prime Minister's eyes were filled with panic. Then he was gone, hustled away to safety by the shouting bodyguards.

Quickly, Tom turned to Rosie. "Are you okay?"

"Yes." She stood by the wall, wide-eyed. The flowers lay on the floor. Tom grabbed Rosie's hand, and ran to the kitchen, where she was safely gathered up in her mother's arms.

All work had stopped in the kitchen. People were shouting questions and staring down the hallway. Then someone came running in with the news: "False alarm! One of those huge balloons exploded. People are calming down—they all thought it was a gunshot."

"Well," someone laughed, "the pep rally is over. The Prime Minister has left the building."

"Where'd he go?"

"Those bodyguards rushed him through the kitchen to a limousine outside. It took off fast with an escort of motorcycle cops."

"Those Mounties weren't taking any chances," Rosie's mother said. "They sure got the PM out fast."

"Dunbar panicked," Tom said. "He was really scared."

"I doubt it," scoffed one of the bakery chefs. "Dunbar isn't afraid of anything. He was a college football star."

"That's right," said Rosie's mother. "Then he was offered a contract to play pro ball—Dallas wanted him." She smacked her fist into a fat roll of dough. "But he went into politics instead. The man is gorgeous—a natural. Everyone thinks he's number one."

"My Mom doesn't," Tom replied. "She says . . . "

"Hey!" The junior chef snapped his fingers at Tom. "You with the red hair—get back to work. You're too fond of talking."

Tom reluctantly lowered his hands into the greasy water. "I don't care what anyone thinks," he said to himself. "The Prime Minister is a coward."

An hour later, the bodyguards returned for Tom.

2

The bodyguards showed their RCMP photo ID cards, explained their reasons, and then hurried Tom outside. It was March, and the air was cold. A black limousine was waiting at the curb. The engine purred.

Inside the limo, a man in his thirties sat on the back seat. His overcoat looked expensive; his circular eyeglasses were the latest style. "I'm Blake Decker," he said to Tom. "Mr. Decker to you. I'm chief adviser to the Prime Minister."

He gestured at Tom to sit beside him. A Mountie climbed in and sat nearby on a folding seat. The limousine pulled smoothly away from the curb and gathered speed.

Tom looked at Blake Decker. "These officers said the Prime Minister wants to see me."

The man's lips curled in a thin smile. "For some

reason, the PM told me to find out the name of the kid with the red hair. You were in the hallway when the bodyguards rushed him out, right?"

Tom nodded.

"Well," Decker shrugged, "it's something about that."

Tom looked through the smoky windows at passing lights. He remembered riding in a limousine through Québec City and a girl he'd met in Baie St-Paul. He missed Michelle.

The Mountie said, "Your father's Inspector Ted Austen of the Winnipeg City Police?"

Tom nodded, still thinking about Michelle.

"He's a nice guy. I'm working with him on security for the Prime Minister's visit."

"I'm thinking of joining the Canadian Security Intelligence Service," Tom said. "When I'm older."

"CSIS, eh? That could be exciting."

"It's like being a spy, right?" Tom's sky-blue eyes shone. "I read a book by an ex-CSIS agent. She travelled to all kinds of places, investigating threats to Canadian security. What a life!"

Soon after, the limousine stopped at the canopied entrance of an exclusive Winnipeg hotel. In the lobby, chandeliers sparkled far above the marble floor. People turned to stare at Tom and the bodyguards as Blake Decker led the way to a bank of elevators.

As they rose toward the upper floors, Tom checked his hair in a mirror. "Will the media be present when I meet the Prime Minister?"

"No—this is strictly private." Decker looked at Tom. "Your generation is so lucky, kid. U-SAC will change your lives. I should show you the flag I've designed for the new country."

Tom said nothing.

"Listen, kid, your parents are voting yes to U-SAC. Correct?"

Tom shook his head. "They're against it."

Blake Decker snorted angrily. "Every opinion poll indicates that U-SAC has huge support among the population—huge. Your parents are being foolish."

The elevator doors hissed open. A long hallway, carpeted in red, led to a cream-coloured door. On it, brass letters read, *The Louis Riel Suite*. Two Mounties guarded the door. One held up a hand as Tom approached. "I'll have to frisk you, sonny."

The search was quick and professional. "The kid's clean," the Mountie said to Decker. "You can go inside."

Prime Minister James Dunbar was pacing the floor of the suite's very large living room. He was in shirt-sleeves, with his silk tie pulled open at the throat. Tiny halogen beams gleamed on expensive paintings, and large windows displayed the city's twinkling lights. High in the black sky, a plane moved past.

The Prime Minister crossed the room to Tom. Close up, his eyes were a startling blue. "Hi there, Tom!" His voice was a deep baritone; his smile revealed perfect teeth. A powerful handshake made Tom wince. "I'm your Prime Minister. But I guess you know that!"

Tom nodded.

"It's nice of you to visit, Tom. What'll you drink— Coke? Pepsi?"

"Canada Dry, if you've got it. Thanks."

Prime Minister Dunbar glanced at Blake Decker. "Get the kid a drink."

The aide disappeared into the suite's kitchen. "So," the Prime Minister said to Tom, "that was pretty exciting today, right? We all thought someone was shooting." He laughed heartily. "We were wrong about that!"

Tom said nothing. Decker returned with his drink; it bubbled and fizzed in a crystal glass.

"That little girl wasn't hurt," the Prime Minister said. "I had someone find out." He paused, thinking. Blake Decker watched him intently. "So, Tom," the Prime Minister continued, "I'm wondering what you remember about that moment."

"Moment?"

"When someone tripped me, and I fell forward. Don't you remember, Tom? I accidentally knocked that little girl aside. That's how you remember it, Tom. Correct?"

"I . . ."

"I've learned some information about your family, Tom. Your mother is a Winnipeg lawyer, right? I can arrange for her to get some government contracts. The money's very good." Again, the Prime Minister displayed his perfect teeth in a large smile. "It was an accident. Right, Tom?"

The telephone rang. Decker picked it up and began a conversation. "It's good to hear your voice, Ashley," he said. "You've arrived in town safely? Where are you staying?" Decker jotted a note. "JBI-306, correct? Okay, I'll see you soon." He hung up the phone.

Almost immediately, it rang again. "It's a call from the lobby," Decker reported to the Prime Minister. "Your father just arrived at the hotel. He's coming up to see you."

The Prime Minister groaned. "My father! That's all I need." He looked at Blake Decker. "I had dinner with him last night—that was enough. Get rid of him, Decker."

"Yes, sir."

"I can't take another evening of his complaints." Kicking off his Guccis, the Prime Minister sprawled on the sofa and stared moodily at the night sky. "I made it to the top—all the way to Prime Minister— and Father still doesn't respect me. Tell me, Decker, why should I waste any more time hearing about my failings? The man never approved of me—never!"

"I'll take care of him, sir."

As Blake Decker walked to the door, Tom quickly followed.

"Good night," he said over his shoulder.

"Remember one thing," the Prime Minister called to Tom. "If you sell your story to the media, your mother won't get any government contracts."

Tom didn't reply.

In the hallway, Blake Decker studied Tom's face as they walked toward the elevators. "So, Tom, what actually happened in that hallway? Did the PM slap the kid, or something like that?"

Tom remained silent. He pushed the elevator button, impatient to leave.

"Don't go yet," Decker said. "I could move a bit of cash your way." He touched his pocket. "I've got a few bills in my wallet. Just tell me, Tom, what happened in that hallway?"

The elevator doors opened. Tom saw a sad-eyed older man in a motorized wheelchair. He was terribly thin, and his fingers were yellow with nicotine. His beard and hair were grey.

Blake Decker spread his arms wide. "Professor Dunbar! What a pleasure to see you, sir."

The professor's wheelchair rolled out of the elevator. The doors closed. "I'm here to see my son," Professor Dunbar said. "The matter is urgent." Suddenly, he bent forward, coughing and hacking.

Blake Decker watched him suffer, then said, "Sir, I have bad news. Today at the convention centre there was a serious incident."

"Someone tried to kill my son?"

"Something like that," Decker replied. "So he's taken a pill and gone to bed early. Doctor's orders. I know you'll understand."

"But this is a serious matter!" Again Professor Dunbar was shaken by terrible coughing. When the fit was over, he leaned back in his wheelchair and whispered, "I'd give anything for a cigarette right now."

"An urgent matter, professor? What's it about?"

Decker led the professor down the hallway. They began speaking in heated whispers. Tom moved a few paces closer, straining to hear. Shaking his finger in Decker's face, the professor said something about *CanSell* and *disgraceful* and *media outrage*.

Blake Decker's face revealed nothing as the men returned to the elevators. "I'll arrange a breakfast meeting tomorrow," Decker said politely to Professor Dunbar. "7:00 A.M., sharp. The PM will make you feel better, I'm sure. What you've heard about him is an ugly rumour, nothing more."

Tom and the professor entered the elevator. As the

doors slipped together, Tom had a final look at Blake Decker. He was lost in thought, with a worried frown on his face.

* * *

As the elevator descended, Professor Dunbar introduced himself. "I teach anthropology at the University of Manitoba," the man said. "I have a special interest in the Arctic regions."

"That's a coincidence," Tom replied. "Next week, some kids from the Arctic are visiting here. It's a school exchange. We'll be doing lots of great things together. We've booked the James Bay Inn for the farewell banquet."

"Bring them to see the university." The professor coughed badly. "Come to a lecture—it's a bit like a class in school, but with lots more students. My topic this month is Arctic explorers. Some died horrible deaths." For a moment he was lost in thought. Then he looked up at Tom. "So—what do you think of U-SAC?"

"I . . . "

"I don't like it," the professor declared. "U-SAC is not for the good of Canadians—it will only benefit special interest groups. To them, U-SAC is a great way to make big money." He stared moodily at his yellow fingertips. "My son knows it's true."

"Maybe the U-SAC referendum will be defeated, Professor Dunbar."

"Only by a miracle," the professor said, as the doors opened onto the lobby. "And I don't believe in miracles."

3

The next morning, Tom was drinking orange juice at the kitchen counter. His mother came into the room, yawning. She was in her dressing gown, and her long red hair wasn't yet combed.

"I was in court all day yesterday," she said to Tom, "then I worked on legal briefs at the office until midnight. How was your dishwashing job?"

"Disgusting!"

Mrs. Austen chuckled. "Welcome to the real world."

"But something happened, Mom." Tom described in detail the events of the evening. "The Prime Minister offered me a bribe to keep quiet! Isn't that against the law?"

"No. Prime Minister Dunbar was inside the law, but only just. Clearly, he's frightened of looking bad. I'm not surprised. The media will make a sensation out of anything—scandals sell big-time. No wonder some people won't go into politics."

"By the way, Mom, I won't be selling my story."

"Thanks for telling me," she said with a smile, "but I already knew that."

Mrs. Austen switched on the television. "This country has had some great prime ministers, and we'll have more of them. But James Dunbar is a disaster. He wants U-SAC to succeed so he can make a personal fortune. I've heard some scary rumours."

On the news, the Prime Minister was seen boarding a flight to Regina. Blake Decker was beside him, looking unhappy. His sallow face was no match for the Prime Minister's movie star looks.

"The pre-dawn flight was a change in plans," the announcer said. "Although the Prime Minister left Winnipeg earlier than scheduled, he'll stop here briefly next week for a visit with his father. Then he heads to the Maritime provinces, where he'll speak in support of U-SAC."

Mrs. Austen turned down the volume. "We need leaders who are loyal to the country and the people. Not Dunbar with his greed."

She sweetened her coffee with honey. "I heard the Prime Minister has a secret deal with a hush-hush consortium code-named CanSell. This company wants to build huge dams to change the direction of some Canadian rivers so that they'll flow through canals to the southern United States. I understand a few states are getting desperate for new sources of water."

"The professor mentioned the name CanSell when he was talking to Blake Decker."

"Without a border, CanSell's diversion project has a much stronger chance of getting government approval." Mrs. Austen sipped her coffee. "Anyway, that's what people are saying. But there's no proof."

Liz joined them. She was dressed for school, and had her materials neatly organized. "I made you a lunch, Tom."

"Great—thanks!"

As Liz helped herself to oat bran from the stove, Inspector Austen phoned from police headquarters to say hello. He'd worked long hours on the security for the Prime Minister's visit. "Are you looking forward to your guests from up north?" he asked Tom.

"Sure, Dad. We're taking them to Chinatown tonight, then we're going bowling. Know what? Someone said they've never seen trees before."

"You've never seen an igloo, son. So it's a shame you're not going to the Arctic with your class. It's a once-in-a-lifetime chance."

"I know, Dad, but I already told you the reason. My team's got a major tournament the same time as the trip north. The coach says I've got to play. Otherwise, he'll bench me for the playoffs."

"Why's this particular tournament so important?"

"The coach's son is our goalie. He's excellent. NHL scouts will be at the tournament. The coach wants his strongest possible team on the ice, to help his son's chances."

"Well, it's a shame."

"I know, Dad, but that's life."

* * *

A few days later, the Winnipeg airport buzzed with conversation. Tom's friends from his Grade Nine class were waiting to greet the visitors from Gjoa Haven in the Arctic. Among the waiting students was Dietmar Oban, whose name was pronounced Deet-mar. Hands in his pockets, he was staring gloomily at the floor.

"More trouble at home?" Tom asked.

Dietmar nodded slowly. "Sometimes, I want to smash every bottle in the house. Maybe then my Dad would quit with the booze."

"Here they are," cried an excited voice. The class pressed forward to greet the northern teenagers. Huddled together in parkas with colourful fringes, the visitors gazed shyly at the waiting crowd.

Dietmar shook hands with twins—a boy and girl. They had raven-black hair. "Welcome to Winnipeg," Dietmar said, introducing himself and Tom. "You'll be staying at my house."

"I'm Rachel," the girl said shyly. "This is my brother, Moses." She handed Dietmar a pin with an image of an Inuk out fishing on a frozen day. It read, *The Hamlet of Gjoa Haven*.

"The lucky guy," Tom said, studying the pin. "I wish I was going north to try ice fishing, and it would have been fun to have someone stay at my house during your visit to Winnipeg."

Moses presented Dietmar with a small carving. "I made this for you," he said quietly. Then he stared at the terminal's high ceiling. Suspended far above was a single-seater biplane with yellow wings. "Man, this place is so huge. I can't believe my eyes."

Dietmar gave the twins souvenir pins of Winnipeg's

famous Golden Boy statue. "Come on, I'll introduce you around."

People stood in groups, waiting for the luggage. Some talked and laughed; others were quiet. Tom was introduced to Constance and Frieda, two friendly teachers from Gjoa Haven. "Call us by our first names," Constance said with a smile. "We're very informal up north."

Someone touched Tom's shoulder. He saw a muscular little man with brown hair cropped close to the scalp and piercing green eyes. He was chewing gum. "I'm Luke Yates," the man said. "Call me Luke." He parked his gum behind an ear. "I'm a freelance writer. I'm on assignment for a newspaper called News/North. They're paying me to report on the visit of these northern kids to Winnipeg. It's good money, but a lousy assignment."

"Why's that?" Tom asked.

Yates glanced at the twins. "I'll tell you another time." He opened a notepad. "So, how's it feel being visited by a bunch of Eskimos?"

Before Tom could answer, they were joined by two more adults from the north. One was an Inuk with a strong face, large eyes, and black hair that gleamed under the airport lights. The second man looked unhealthy. Behind old-fashioned spectacles, he had watery blue eyes; his skin was very pale. A few days worth of blond bristles outlined his jaw and chin.

The blond man spoke to the writer. "I'm Sam White. Is there a problem here?"

"Not at all, mister. I'm on assignment for a newspaper, so I'm interviewing these Eskimos."

"A writer? Then why so ignorant?" Sam poked Luke Yates in the chest. "Let me tell you something, sir. The word Eskimo means eater of raw flesh, and is considered an insult. My friends appreciate being called Inuit, which simply means people. Now, leave them alone, okay, and leave me alone, too."

Shaking his head, Luke Yates walked away. As he did, Sam turned to the Inuk. "You okay, Junior?"

"I'm fine," Junior replied. "I've met people like him before."

"It's a poor start to our visit," Sam said. "That guy acts racist. He'd better not cause any trouble."

* * *

The next day, the sightseeing northerners and their hosts arrived at the University of Manitoba, just south of Winnipeg. The visitors had asked to see real farm animals, and they were also looking forward to Professor Dunbar's lecture about the Arctic. Several teachers were with them, and so was Luke Yates. The freelance writer carried a camera and his notepad.

The campus had many different buildings; students hurried between them, their breath turning white in the cold air. After taking some photos outside the administration building, the group walked across campus toward the Faculty of Agriculture. Tom was with Junior and Junior's father, who were both chaperons from the Arctic. Junior's father was taking a holiday from his duties as the Mountie in Gjoa Haven to be a volunteer on the trip south.

The group reached one of the barns where research was conducted to help farmers. It was filled with the cackles, bellows, and whinnies of many animals. Moses covered his nose. "That smell is so strong!"

"Look!" Rachel pointed across the barn. Her eyes were huge. "Look at that—a horse, a real horse!"

Dietmar smiled at her. "It seems amazing you've never seen farm animals before."

"I wish I could ride it. On TV, horses look like fun."

Soon after, they entered Tache Hall. The building was jammed with students. On one colourful wall, a poster proclaimed, *If you can read this, thank a teacher*. Listening in on conversations, Tom heard discussions about lectures and parties and movies and someone's missing wallet.

"I hated that course," one student said, "it was extreme torture."

"You did all that work? You keener, you."

"The prof had, like, all this curly, curly hair but he shaved it off."

"See that guy? He knows how to juggle. I mean, that's so cool."

Tom grinned at Dietmar. "What a bunch of characters! If a crime happened here, there'd be some great suspects."

Dietmar winked at Rachel. "I've suffered this detective nonsense since we were kids. Austen will never grow up."

"I hope not," she replied, favoring Tom with a pretty smile.

"Hey," Dietmar said, frowning. "I hope you don't *like* Austen, Rachel. His taste in music is the pits."

"What's wrong with Elvis?" Tom asked.

"Come on!" Dietmar groaned.

Inside a lecture hall, they found hundreds of seats rising all around in a horseshoe pattern. Students were reading textbooks, making notes, and gossiping together as they awaited the arrival of Professor Dunbar.

"So many people," Rachel said as they were directed to reserved seats.

Tom sat beside Sam and his girlfriend, Faith. Her hair and eyes were the same beautiful black as the other northerners. Faith was exceptionally quiet, and seemed on edge. City noises made her jump nervously.

"How'd you end up in the Arctic?" Tom asked Sam.

"I served with Junior in the same army unit. Later I went north to visit him, and fell in love with Faith." He smiled at her. "Since then, the Arctic has been home. It's paradise to me."

Faith kissed Sam's cheek. "I'm glad you decided to come on this trip."

"It was a last-minute decision," he said to Tom, "but I don't regret it. Winnipeg's a fun city." Sam wiped his watery eyes. "I wish you'd try a different perfume, Faith. My allergy's real bad today."

She looked at him, but said nothing.

Sam smiled at Tom. "I hope you'll enjoy our town, when your class visits."

"Unfortunately," Tom replied, "I'm not going north. I'm playing hockey instead."

"You're the lucky one," Dietmar said. "I'm dreading this trip. Snow and cold and frostbite—ugh."

At that moment, Professor Dunbar appeared on a small stage in his motorized wheelchair. Dark circles lined his tired eyes. "Did the prof sleep in that sweater?" Dietmar whispered. "He looks terrible."

Faith leaned close to them. "Guess what? The professor is going to die."

4

Sam smiled. "We're all going to die, sweetheart."

"No, I mean *soon*. Professor Dunbar is dying."

Tom was shocked by the news. "What do you mean?"

"See those students?" Faith glanced at a group of young women chatting together. "I just heard them talking. The professor has terminal lung cancer." She turned to Sam. "It proves what I've been saying, sweetheart. People with addictions are asking for trouble."

"Well . . . "

The professor switched on a microphone, and everyone fell silent. The students waited with their pens, ready to make notes.

"Today . . . " A hacking cough shook Professor Dunbar's body. "Today is special. Our guests are from the Arctic—please welcome them." As applause rang out, the northern visitors smiled with shy eyes.

The professor looked at some of the Winnipeg teens. "The Arctic is a fabulous land—the place of dreams and drama. Put away your video games, for this is the ultimate adventure." He then began a fascinating lecture on Arctic explorers; although racked by coughing, Professor Dunbar spoke for an hour while his students wrote busily.

"Finally," he said, "I want you to imagine today's astronauts disappearing without a trace while exploring the moon. You can guess what the uproar would be back home! Well, that's exactly what happened in the nineteenth century when the British explorer Sir James Franklin and 128 men vanished while attempting to become the first Europeans to travel across the top of Canada by sea. They were searching for the fabled Northwest Passage."

A severe bout of coughing shook Professor Dunbar's body. "Like many men, Franklin assumed he knew everything. While exploring the Arctic, he thought there was nothing to learn from the Inuit— even though they'd lived successfully for centuries in the harsh northern climate! His vessel carried china and silverware and over a thousand books, but precious little that could be of real help when the two British ships were trapped by ice."

Professor Dunbar looked around the lecture hall. "The Franklin expedition ended in tragedy. The British ignored the Inuit, who could have helped them survive. The sailors tried to walk to safety—without any snowshoes and wearing canvas coats instead of caribou skins. Starving, they were forced to eat the flesh of their dead friends."

He paused. "Every man perished; 138 years later, anthropologist Owen Beattie from the University of Alberta discovered three coffins on Beechey Island. Inside were the bodies of young English sailors, perfectly preserved by the bitter cold."

The professor touched a switch. Projected on a screen was the face of a dead sailor. "Dr. Beattie took this picture of James Torrington. He was 20 years old when he died on New Year's Day, 1846."

The sailor's eyes stared from their sockets. His nose was black, and so were his lips. His mouth was frozen open; he wore a striped shirt with mother-of-pearl buttons. "This is beyond gross," Dietmar moaned, gazing in horror at the screen. "I'm never going to the Arctic. Never."

"Those young men needn't have suffered such a fate," cried the professor. "They died because their commander, the famous Sir James Franklin, did not respect the Inuit. Are we any different today? I hope so."

He looked at his northern guests. "We would do well to listen to your ancient civilization. We have much to learn from your wisdom."

As the university students applauded enthusiastically, the professor slumped back in his wheelchair, coughing horribly. After wiping a weary hand across his face, he left the stage.

Sam looked at his Rolex. "I'm hungry. Let's eat something."

Dietmar grinned at him. "You think like me—with your stomach."

After eating lunch in the cafeteria, the teens and adults sat talking at large tables. Alone in a corner, Luke Yates scribbled notes.

"What did you think of the lecture?" Tom called to the writer.

"It was garbage," snarled Yates, without looking up. "That prof is a fool."

Sam went in search of the washroom. The moment he was gone, Faith and Junior moved to another table and began talking in low voices. Tom couldn't hear their discussion.

"Okay if I take off for a few minutes?" he asked his teacher. "I'd like to find Professor Dunbar's office, and thank him. It was nice of him to invite us today."

"Good thinking, Tom. But hurry back, please. Don't start looking for some major villainy to investigate."

Tom smiled. "Crime at a university, sir? I doubt it!"

* * *

A student in a jaunty black beret directed Tom to a staircase. "You'll find Professor Dunbar's office on the second floor."

The hallway was lined with doors. On one, a nameplate read, *Professor Lionel Dunbar*. The door, like the Austens' refrigerator at home, was covered with witty cartoons and interesting items clipped from newspapers. Through a small window, Tom saw the professor's office. It was cluttered with books, books, and more books.

When Tom knocked, a voice called, "Enter!" Inside, Tom noticed that several news clippings had been thrown into the professor's waste basket. They were about his son, Prime Minister James Dunbar.

The office contained a sofa and easy chair, plus a large desk and high-tech work station. A door led to a small private washroom. The floor-to-ceiling bookcases contained many titles about the Arctic. Tom moved closer to the window, wishing the professor would open it; the air reeked of stale tobacco.

Outside, he could see Luke Yates standing under the bare branches of an elm. He was smoking a cigarette, and staring moodily into space. Tom looked at him briefly, and then said, "We all enjoyed the lecture, Professor Dunbar. I came to say thanks for the invitation."

The professor smiled, and for a moment the sadness left his eyes. "It's good to see you, Tom." He was shaken by terrible coughing. "Let me show you some interesting photos of the Arctic. You're going to love your visit to Gjoa Haven."

"Unfortunately," Tom replied, "I'm not going."

"What a shame."

Professor Dunbar went to his desk and eyed the red numerals on a small box. When the digits reached 00:00, a cigarette rolled out. "This box dispenses one an hour," the professor explained, grabbing the cigarette and a lighter. He dragged heavily, then his body was racked by appalling coughs and hacks.

Tom examined a picture on the wall. "Is this the *St. Roch*? We studied it in school."

The professor finished his cigarette and coughed again before replying. "Yes, that's the RCMP's famous schooner. Imagine the adventure, Tom Austen. Valiant Mounties in a wooden boat, braving the Arctic ice.

They were the first to circumnavigate North America. These days, cruise ships make the same journey—but the *St. Roch* was wooden-hulled, and tiny by comparison. It would almost fit into one of those ships' swimming pools."

Tom walked to the window. No one stood by the elm tree. Where had Luke Yates gone?

"Listen, Professor Dunbar, can you give me some inside information on Roald Amundsen? I'm writing a report on him for school."

The professor rolled to another picture. "This is Amundsen, the Norwegian who was the first European to get through the legendary passage. He trained hard before making the attempt. But it was worth it—his childhood dream came true." The professor glanced at the wastepaper basket, sighing. "I'm sure his father was proud."

"Is that his boat? It's so small."

"You're right, Tom. It was originally used to fish for herring. Amundsen wanted a craft that could sneak between drifting ice floes." Professor Dunbar leaned forward in his wheelchair, coughing painfully. "Roald Amundsen wasn't a snob like Franklin. He put on caribou skins, he travelled light. He learned from the Inuit."

"What was his boat called?" Tom asked.

"The *Gjoa*. During his voyage, Amundsen wintered on King William Island at Gjoa Haven. Hence the community's name." The professor's brown eyes turned longingly to the digital readout, but his next cigarette wouldn't arrive for 56 minutes.

"Professor Dunbar, may I use your washroom?"

"Of course."

Stepping into the washroom, Tom closed the door. There were no windows; a fluorescent light glared over the sink. He was drying his hands when he heard a knocking sound. "Enter!" cried the professor.

"Blake Decker?" Professor Dunbar sounded surprised. "You're here? But why—I don't understand. Is it about my dinner tonight with James? Surely my son hasn't cancelled!"

Tom stayed motionless. He heard the outside door close. "Nice office, professor," said the smooth voice of the Prime Minister's aide, Blake Decker. "It stinks of cigarettes, though."

"What do you want, Decker? And who's this?"

"You may call this person ZULU-1. I decided to bring some muscle, in case you get difficult."

"Why are you here, Decker?"

"What have you learned about CanSell, Professor?"

"CanSell is the code name for a secret plan to sell water from Canadian rivers." The professor sounded angry. "A good friend called me from Washington, D.C. He said James has been promised a fortune if he can advance CanSell's secret plans by getting Canada to join the USA. I'll demand answers when I see James tonight. If it's true, I'll go straight to the media. The Canadian people must know the truth about their Prime Minister."

"Your friend in Washington is correct," said Blake Decker. "It's all true about CanSell—and I should know. I'm involved myself."

"Just as I feared. So James is controlled by CanSell?"

"Yes."

"My son, my son! A traitor to his nation!" The

professor hacked and coughed terribly. "My heart is broken. What will I say to the media?"

"Don't worry about that, Professor. You won't be talking to the media. You'll be dead." Blake Decker's voice was low and ominous. "Okay ZULU-1, it's time. Use the silencer."

"No," the professor cried. "You can't . . . "

A sharp SNAP of sound was followed by a terrible crash, and then moaning that made Tom's scalp creep. He leaned close to the door, terrified.

"A clean shot," Blake Decker said. "You got him through the heart. The professor is dead."

* * *

Tom stared into the washroom mirror. His skin was chalk-white, his eyes enormous. Inside his chest was a terrible pounding.

"I'll phone the Prime Minister on his private line," said Blake Decker. "He didn't like his father, but he'll still be shocked." He chuckled.

A few moments later, Decker said, "Prime Minister? Decker here." There was a brief pause. "I know you're entertaining VIPs, but I've got important news. Your father's been shot dead." The aide's voice had a sharp edge to it. "Now, listen. I arranged the hit, so you're involved. If I'm ever arrested, they'll get you, too."

A long silence. Then Decker said, "We must cover up the truth about your father's death. Otherwise, you're finished, U-SAC is finished, and CanSell is finished. We don't want that, correct?"

Tom was frozen. He was certain his heart could be heard through the door.

"A good decision, Prime Minister. I agree, let's cover it up. I'll take your father's wallet so the police will think a thief shot him. His death won't be connected to you."

A pause.

"Don't worry, Prime Minister. The truth won't come out. I'll be in touch soon. Goodbye."

Tom heard Decker hang up the phone. Then the man laughed. "See this micro-cassette, ZULU-1? I just used the telephone answering machine to record the Prime Minister ordering a cover-up. I'll edit out my voice, then play him the tape and threaten to release it to the media. He'll be terrified. This gives me absolute control over the Prime Minister. I can make him do anything—I'm going to be a very wealthy man."

Again a chuckle. "We'd better get moving. But first I'll use that washroom."

Tom was horrified. His eyes darted around, seeking escape, but he was trapped.

5

The doorknob rattled. "It's locked," said Blake Decker. "I wonder if there's someone . . . " Then he exclaimed, "Look—through the window! A campus police car, heading this way. Let's get out of here."

Tom remained paralyzed until he heard help arrive. Rushing out of hiding, he saw two university police officers kneeling over the professor. His body lay sprawled on the carpet next to the forlorn sight of the fallen wheelchair.

An officer stared at Tom. "Who are you?" she demanded.

"I heard everything," Tom exclaimed. "The Prime Minister is involved! Is the professor dead for sure?"

The second officer nodded. "He had a weak heart and was in danger of having a heart attack, so he wore a warning alert system linked to our headquarters. It triggered an alarm a few minutes ago, at the moment he was shot, I guess."

The officers called city police for emergency backup, and requested an APB for the arrest of Blake Decker. Then they began taking a witness statement from Tom. To his dismay, he learned that his evidence against James Dunbar could not be used in court.

"It's called hearsay," one officer explained. "There's no proof of what you heard. The Prime Minister would claim innocence."

"Also remember," the second officer told Tom, "you only heard Blake Decker on the phone. Maybe he was pretending to speak to the Prime Minister."

"I doubt it," Tom said grimly. "James Dunbar ordered a cover-up of his father's murder."

"That's a major accusation, young man. You need proof."

"It exists," Tom replied. "If that micro-cassette can be found, the Prime Minister is finished."

"There'll be a full investigation, of course. Now, tell us more about ZULU-1. Did you hear him speak?"

"Never. Which means the person could have been a woman."

"Good point. Now—think back to the hallway outside the professor's office. Did you notice anything suspicious?"

Tom shook his head. "The hallway was empty. I didn't see anyone there, but . . . ."

Feet were heard in the hallway. "Someone's coming," an officer said, "running fast. I wonder who?" He went to the door. "Keep back. I'll deal with this."

The officer switched off the lights, and the room went

dark. He stepped into the hallway. Through the window in the door, Tom saw Luke Yates come running up.

"Is there trouble here?" Yates demanded. "I was listening to police calls on my radio scanner, and I intercepted your request for backup. This is Professor Dunbar's office, right? He's the Prime Minister's father, right? So what's the story—what's going on?"

"No comment," replied the officer.

"Listen, I'm a freelance writer. I make money by finding important news. I smell a big story here, and that means big money. Let me in that office."

The officer blocked the door with his large body. "Not a chance, mister. There's a witness inside. His identity must be protected."

"A witness?" said Luke Yates. "A witness to what?"

"Murder."

"*What?* Who's dead—the professor?" Luke Yates stared at the officer. "I gotta find a phone! The media will pay huge for this story." He rushed away.

The officer returned inside. "We should move this kid away from here. He could be in danger."

"It was a mistake to mention a witness," the second officer pointed out. "If Blake Decker realizes he can be identified, he'll go into hiding."

"You're right. But it's too late now."

* * *

From the time of the murder, Tom slept uneasily. In his nightmares, he relived the professor's cry of horror. His evidence had been classified by the Winnipeg police, and his identity as a possible witness was also a secret, but he still felt nervous—especially when he thought about Blake Decker.

Unfortunately, the media had quickly spread the news about a witness to the murder, and Decker had disappeared. An extensive police investigation had failed to find his hiding place, to the outrage of news commentators. Some suggested that senior investigators like Inspector Ted Austen should be fired—making for gloomy faces at the Austen household.

On the final evening of the Arctic guests' visit, a farewell banquet was held at the James Bay Inn, a classic small hotel in a residential area of Winnipeg. Tom arrived with Dietmar and his guests, Rachel and Moses. They stood outside, under the hotel's cheerful lights, waiting for the others to arrive.

"The Prime Minister was on the news," Dietmar said. "At his father's funeral."

"I saw him," Tom said. "He was crying crocodile tears."

"What's that mean?" Rachel asked.

"When a crocodile is eating its prey, big tears roll from its eyes. But the croc's not crying for the victim—it's happy."

"How's that connected to Prime Minister Dunbar?"

"I can't tell you," Tom said unhappily. The PM's possible link to the murder remained a secret; the public only knew of the involvement of Blake Decker and ZULU-1.

"I felt sorry for Dunbar at the funeral," Dietmar said. "If I was old enough, I'd vote for U-SAC. It's a good deal for Canada. I hate those long, boring waits at the border crossing. They ruin trips to the States."

"Then stay home," Tom growled, "and spend your money here. It keeps Canadians working."

"Who cares about work?" Grinning, Dietmar put his arm around Rachel. "I just want to party."

When the others arrived, everyone went inside. The hotel's dining room was decorated with colourful balloons and large banners. Photos on one wall showed highlights of the visit by the Gjoa Haven teens.

"I like this one," Moses said to Tom. "It shows our volleyball game against your school."

"We didn't have a chance," Tom lamented. "Your serve is wicked, and so is Rachel's. How come you're so good?"

Moses shrugged. "In the middle of our winter, the sun never rises. It's eternal darkness, 24 hours. Some people hibernate, but not us kids. We play hockey, volleyball, basketball, hour after hour."

They sat down at a long table decorated with flowers. Rachel and Dietmar joined them, along with Joey and Stephanie Villeneuve from Tom's class.

"Still in the detective business, Tom?" Stephanie asked. "What's the latest?"

"I've developed a new message system. You send a sentence that makes no sense. But, secretly, the first letter of each word forms a message."

"For example," Dietmar interrupted, "a spy sends the mysterious message, TRAVEL ON MOST ICE SEES ANIMALS LITTLE OR SMALL ENJOYING RAINBOWS. What's the code's secret meaning?"

"Let's see," Stephanie said, writing on a paper napkin, "T . . . O . . . "

Dietmar grinned. "The code reads TOM IS A LOSER."

"Oban wasn't born," Tom commented, "he was hatched in a lab. Too bad the experiment failed."

Everyone laughed. Then Joey turned to Rachel. "I saw pictures of the carvings Moses has done. They're wonderful."

Rachel nodded. "I think Moses will be a famous artist."

Moses smiled proudly at his sister. "Rachel will lead our people," he said to the others. "She speaks three languages, and she's always studying."

"I am gathering the wisdom of our elders," Rachel said shyly. "So much has changed during their lifetime. As children, the elders lived in snow houses and hunted on the land. Now our people live in settlements, with little hunting or other work. Many young people in the north kill themselves. I want to give hope to kids in despair."

Stephanie's eyes were solemn. "What will you do?"

"First, we must understand the system. That is why I stay in school. For many years, all decisions were made for us by government *kabloonas* from the south. Now my people control Nunavut, which is our homeland. This gives real hope for the future."

"What's a *kabloona*?" Tom asked.

"A white person—it means *man with bushy eyebrows*. There is a legend about my grandfather. As a little boy, he saw *kabloonas* arriving in a boat and ran away, thinking they were ghosts because of their white skin."

"Homeland is a nice word," Dietmar said. "It sounds peaceful, just like a home should be."

"I wish I was going north," Tom said. "I feel like skipping that hockey tournament."

"I'm the opposite," Dietmar commented. "I'd give anything to miss the trip."

"But why? Don't you want to see Rachel again?"

"Of course I do, Austen. But I hate being cold, and Arctic winters are legendary. Up there people freeze solid, all the time."

Rachel giggled. "It's not *that* bad, Dietmar."

He shuddered. "I'll have ice in my underwear."

Moses laughed. "You're so paranoid."

"We studied a poem called 'The Cremation of Sam McGee.' That poor guy was *so* cold. I've never forgotten."

Sam and Faith approached their table, holding hands. Sam smiled. His eyes looked bad, and his nose was dribbling. "Okay to join you?"

"Sure," Tom replied. "Too bad you're leaving tomorrow. I'll miss you guys."

"You're not going to visit Gjoa Haven?" Sam asked.

Tom shook his head. "Unfortunately, no. Maybe I'll see the Arctic after I join the Canadian Security Intelligence Service. They've got agents everywhere."

"You're looking at CSIS for a career? Why's that?"

"Being a secret agent would be cool."

Sam smiled. "Well, if you're in CSIS, you'll see the country for sure."

Some other teens came over to the table, followed by the Inuk Mountie and his son, Junior. "Would you please explain something?" Tom asked the Mountie.

"Certainly, Tom."

"What's the difference between 'Inuk' and 'Inuit'?"

"I am glad you are interested." As the Mountie paused to think, Tom studied his brown skin. It was seared and wrinkled by countless hours in extreme weather conditions. "The word 'Inuit' refers to all the people. An 'Inuk' is only one person—or two."

"I'm confused," Dietmar said.

Tom smiled at his friend. "May I have that in writing?"

The Mountie looked at Tom. "I have spoken to your father on the telephone. We discussed his murder investigation."

"Dad's working on it around the clock."

"I saw the Prime Minister on television, at his father's funeral. His comments to the media about the Winnipeg City Police were not favorable."

Tom's temper flared. "That guy is such a hypocrite!"

"One thing is strange," the Mountie said. "The Prime Minister demands action from the police, yet he's stalling on a government inquiry into his father's death."

For the first time, Faith spoke. "Perhaps because his aide Blake Decker was involved."

"What I can't figure out," Sam said, "is why the cops can't locate Decker. He's got to be hiding somewhere."

Tom stared glumly at the table, wishing he could help his Dad by finding Blake Decker, or by identifying the contract killer code-named ZULU-1. Unfortunately, the list of possible suspects was large—anyone who was at the university that day could have been the killer.

Tom felt eyes on him, and saw Faith staring. Then she smiled. Her face was lovely, but troubled. "You were lost in thought, Tom."

Before he could respond, Tom saw Luke Yates enter the dining room. As usual, the muscular little man was full of energy. "Gimme a few quotes about your visit," he said to the Mountie. "I'm faxing my final story to News/North tonight."

"Please, join us for the banquet." The Mountie gestured at the table. "As my guest."

"Not a chance. I just ate." Luke Yates pulled out his notepad. "Now, give me some quotes. Make them good—I'm hoping for extra money from the paper. I've got a hunting trip coming up."

At the head table, the principal of Tom's school called for attention. As she welcomed the students and their chaperons to the event, Luke Yates sat down at another table and made notes.

Steaming food appeared from the kitchen, carried on large trays by young waiters. Tom recognized one of them; he was Liz's current boyfriend. "Hey, Zoltan," he waved, "good to see you!"

The boy gave him a friendly smile.

"He's so cute," Stephanie said. "Liz has all the luck."

Following the meal, the tables were cleared away for dancing. A student from Tom's school set up a music system, and before long an excellent party was in progress. As voices grew noisy and music pounded the air, Luke Yates prowled with his notebook in search of quotes.

Returning from the washroom, Tom stopped in the lobby to talk to Sam. Then he said good night to the Mountie, who was leaving the hotel, and chatted briefly with Junior. Back at the party, Tom found Dietmar picking his teeth with a book of matches.

"Where's Rachel?"

"In the washroom." Dietmar tossed the matches on a table. "That's cheaper than flossing."

Tom laughed. Then he glanced at the matches and his heart froze. On the package were the initials JBI.

"Hey!"

"What now, Austen?"

Picking up the matches, Tom read *Enjoy your stay at the JBI*. "Those initials mean the James Bay Inn."

"Good work, Sherlock."

Still staring at the matches, Tom walked slowly away from Dietmar. He remembered being at the Prime Minister's hotel suite when Blake Decker spoke on the phone to someone named Ashley. They'd agreed to meet at "JBI-306."

Tom broke into a sweat. What if Blake Decker was hiding upstairs, in Room 306 of the James Bay Inn?

* * *

Tom hurried to the kitchen. Zoltan was stacking clean dishes on a shelf. "I saw you dancing, Tom. I tried it once but I quit—I've got two left feet."

"Listen, Zoltan, I need help."

"No problem, my man. What can I do?"

Minutes later, Tom was dressed as a waiter. On his hand, he balanced a tray containing a silver coffee pot, cups, and cutlery. "How do I look?" he asked.

"Nervous, but okay. You'd pass as a room service waiter."

Zoltan led Tom to narrow stairs at the back of the hotel. "Follow these to the third floor. Good luck."

"Remember what I said, Zoltan. If I don't return soon, call 911. Tell Dad I may have located Blake Decker."

"Let's call him now, Tom. Let the police deal with it."

"It's only a theory, Zoltan, and I've got a bad reputation at police headquarters for some bogus suspicions I've had in the past. First, let me check upstairs. I'll pretend I'm delivering room service, and look for signs of Decker. If he's there, the cops can make the arrest."

"But Room 306 hasn't ordered anything."

"I'll say I got the number wrong. I'll ask to use their phone, to find out the correct room. If I spot any signs of Decker, he's finished."

"This could be a mistake."

Tom smiled bravely. "Not a chance."

* * *

Light from old-fashioned lamps shone on wooden doors along the hallway on the third floor. No one was around. Tom forced himself forward. Room 306 was at the far end. As he approached, Tom heard a voice through the door. A man was speaking. Tom crept closer, straining to hear.

"No," the man's voice said. "You can't take the micro north to Joe. The boat is fine for hiding low-level stuff, but this micro is worth a fortune in blackmail. It stays with me."

Tom leaned his head close to the door. The paint was a bright yellow. He'd heard that voice before; it sounded like Blake Decker.

"I said *no*, ZULU-1, and I meant it. Now, here's your final payment for the hit on the professor." Then, suddenly, the man exclaimed, "Hey! What's with the gun?"

A mumbled response.

"Sure!" Decker sounded terrified. "Okay, here—I'll give you the micro-cassette. Just don't shoot! Here— here's the micro. Now put that thing away, *please*."

Then Tom heard a dreadful SNAP, followed by a horrifying cry, and the thump of a body falling to the floor.

* * *

For a moment, Tom was frozen. Then he turned from the door and walked quickly along the hallway. His hand trembled under the heavy tray, and his legs were like rubber. The hallway seemed impossibly long, the service stairs too distant to reach.

Desperate for refuge, Tom knocked on the door of Room 303. From inside, the voice of an elderly woman called, "Be right there!"

Tom listened to footsteps inside 303—the woman was moving slowly toward the door. *Hurry*, he screamed silently. *Please, hurry*!

The door opened, and a friendly face smiled up at Tom. "Yes, young man?"

Somewhere behind him, a door creaked open. Tom glanced at the coffee pot—the hallway was reflected in its curved surface. The image was distorted, but Tom saw the shape of a person sneaking out of Room 306.

"Yes, young man?"

"Uh . . . " Tom glanced at the woman for a brief moment. "Uh, room service . . . "

When he looked at the coffee pot again, the killer was gone. "Ma'am," he said desperately, "call the front desk . . . call the cops . . . there's, there's . . . been a shooting."

"What?"

"Blake Decker's been shot! Please, get help fast!"

* * *

Within minutes, the hallway swarmed with people. The first sirens could be heard in the distance, wailing closer. The hotel manager had been the first person inside Room 306 and had discovered Blake Decker dead; now he was waiting for the police. Dozens of rumours swept along the crowded hallway—then, suddenly, all voices stopped.

Everyone turned to stare at a woman who'd stepped out of the elevator. She was carrying food from a grocery store in plastic bags. Her face registered surprise. "What's happened?"

"There's been a shooting," the manager said. "In your room, Miss Romero."

"Blake," she cried. The bags crashed to the floor as she covered her mouth with both hands. "Someone shot Blake?"

"Blake Decker was a fugitive from justice, Miss Romero. You let him hide in your room?"

"He threatened me!"

The police arrived at that moment, and the spectators lost interest in Miss Romero. Instead, all eyes were on the manager as he opened the door to 306. The victim could not be seen, but Tom glimpsed a homemade flag on the wall. It was the Stars and Stripes, modified slightly by the presence of a single red maple leaf among the stars.

Tom turned to Zoltan, who was one of the onlookers. "Blake Decker told me he'd designed a flag for U-SAC. I guess that's it." He paused. "Decker will never see it flying over Canada, but what about us?"

"It's a depressing thought," Zoltan replied. "Let's hope U-SAC never happens."

6

Two days later, Tom was at the Winnipeg airport with his classmates. They were checking in luggage tagged *Gjoa Haven*.

Everyone was excited. "This is *so* fantastic," Desmond Chan exclaimed. "Hey, it's great you're going with us, Tom."

"Thanks, Des. Deciding to skip the tournament wasn't easy, but now I'm really glad. I just couldn't miss seeing the Arctic."

Dietmar joined them, face gloomy. "I wrote my last will and testament last night. It's in my room. My collection of movies is yours, Austen. Enjoy them with your girlfriends, and think of me occasionally."

"Hey," Desmond said, "I wouldn't mind getting your silk shirts, Dietmar. What do you say?"

Tom glanced at the check-in counter. "See the guy with all the gear? That's Luke Yates, the freelance writer."

"He looks tough," Desmond said. "I bet he works out with weights."

"He's checking in a rifle. This must be the hunting trip he talked about." Tom frowned. "But I wonder—there's a media uproar about the two murders, so you'd think Yates would stay in town. Chase some stories, make some money."

"I'd holiday instead of working," Dietmar said. "Besides, look at you. Instead of staying home to meddle in the murder investigation, you're taking this trip."

"That's true."

Desmond looked at Dietmar. "Know what my Dad says about the north? It's so cold the fillings drop from your teeth. I couldn't tell if he was joking."

Dietmar whimpered.

"You shouldn't be so nervous," Tom said. "I'm not."

"What about the huskies? You're scared of dogs."

"Yeah, well . . . "

"We're going to sleep overnight in *igloos*, Austen! We won't survive, I guarantee it. Make one little mistake in the Arctic and you are toast."

"Correction," Tom said. "You're a polar bear's frozen TV dinner."

The students were herded together for a group picture, and then said goodbye to their families. Mrs. Austen and Liz were present, but Tom's father was busy investigating the murders.

Liz was watching the news on her tiny hand-held television set. Inspector Austen was at a press conference; he was sweating under the glare of lights as reporters yelled questions. "Just because ZULU-1 has vanished," Liz said, "the media's all over the police. It's not fair!"

Next on the news was the latest opinion poll on the referendum. With only ten days left until the vote, almost 70 percent had decided to say yes to union with the United States. Mrs. Austen sighed unhappily as the Prime Minister appeared, beaming at the poll results. "Liz, turn that thing off."

Tom shook his head. "I'm convinced the missing micro-cassette holds the truth about the Prime Minister. Now the killer has it—but who knows where?"

"You couldn't identify ZULU-1 for the police?" Mrs. Austen asked.

Tom shook his head. "I only saw a distorted reflection. ZULU-1 was disguised in a balaclava and overalls. The police found them later, abandoned in the hotel's cellar."

"Tell me again," Mrs. Austen said. "What did Blake Decker say to ZULU-1 in Room 306?"

Tom opened his notebook. "He said—'You can't take the micro north to Joe.' There was also something about hiding it in a boat."

"Finding Joe is the key," Liz said. She handed Tom some miniaturized binoculars. "Makiko gave me these, as a souvenir of St. Andrews. They may be useful up north."

"Thanks, sis."

"I wish you'd take my key ring with the rabbit's foot and four-leaf clover."

Tom smiled. "I'm not superstitious."

Liz hugged her brother goodbye. "Enjoy the meals, but don't choke on the raw seal."

Tom kissed his mother. "Tell Dad to relax. He's so tense these days."

"He'll be okay, honey." Mrs. Austen smiled, but Tom knew she was worried.

* * *

After a smooth flight, their Canadian Airlines jet approached Yellowknife, the north's largest city. After passing hundreds of small lakes, they were descending over Great Slave Lake, which was enormous. The city stood beside it, surrounded by snow-covered trees.

"They've got high-rise buildings," Bonita Vanderveen reported from her window. "And I see a mall!"

Inside the terminal, they assembled for instructions from one of their teachers, Mr. Cousins. "Our next plane leaves in three hours," he announced. "So we'll go into town."

After shopping at the YK Centre, they toured a museum in the heart of the city. "Look at the teeth," Dietmar said, examining an enormous polar bear. "I hear these bears can run incredibly fast."

"Only if they're hungry for an Oban-burger," said Tom, who was studying another display. "Look at this—the saber-toothed cat once roamed the north. Camels, too, and woolly mammoths. They're all extinct, but the musk-oxen still survive up there. They go back two million years. Wouldn't it be something to actually see one?"

"Thrilling, I'm sure."
"Relax, Oban. You'll love the Arctic."
"Sure thing, Austen."

* * *

Back at the airport, they saw Luke Yates waiting for the next flight. Also in the lounge were some Inuit who would be going home to Gjoa Haven on the plane. Dressed in colourful parkas, they sat surrounded by shopping bags and large packages from Tim Hortons Donuts and McDonald's. Their children stopped playing to stare at the teenagers from the south.

Tom sat beside one of his teachers, Mr. Plantinga. "Why've they got all that food, sir?"

"You won't find the golden arches in Gjoa Haven, Tom. These people are returning with treats for their families."

"My Mom forced me to bring a pineapple for my hosts. I feel like an idiot, travelling with a pineapple!"

The teacher smiled. "Good for your mother. Fresh fruit is a delicacy in the Arctic."

Then a familiar person appeared. It was Constance, one of the teachers from Gjoa Haven. "Surprise! First Air kindly flew me down here to welcome you to the north. Everyone's very excited about your visit! You know my husband's an Inuk, eh? You'll be overnighting with him in igloos far from town. It's called going out on the land. The winds blow *really* cold out there!"

Dietmar moaned.

"The people in Gjoa are my family now," Constance said, as she smiled at the Inuit waiting for the flight. "I miss the city, but I'm staying north."

"Excuse me, Constance," Tom said. "Did you just say, 'the people in Joe'? What's that mean?"

"Gjoa is short for Gjoa Haven. Just like Spence means Spence Bay."

"But you pronounce it 'Joe'?" Tom jotted the information in his notebook. "That's really important!" Grabbing Dietmar, he led him away from the others. "I've got a theory."

Dietmar rolled his eyes.

At that moment, a voice announced, *First Air flight 842 now boarding for Gjoa Haven.* "On the plane," Tom promised, "I'll tell you all the details."

"What a thrill awaits me."

* * *

Outside the terminal, they hurried across the snow-blown tarmac toward a turbo-prop displaying the logo of First Air. The space inside was divided between seats for the passengers and a large area for cargo.

"What are you taking north?" Mr. Cousins asked the friendly flight attendant.

"Fresh eggs, new movies, snowmobile parts, a shortwave radio. All the essentials of life."

The Hawker-Siddley HS 748 bumped along the runway and then roared into the air. "So long, Yellow-knife," Dietmar said mournfully, looking down from his window. "Farewell to civilization."

"Relax, Oban." Tom glanced across the aisle at Luke Yates, who sat alone, loudly chewing gum. The writer was studying an ad for high-power rifles in a magazine for hunters. "Listen to the noise he's making. Disgusting."

"You're so neurotic, Austen."

"He's got a bottle of rum hidden inside his coat. I saw him take a drink."

The flight attendant welcomed them on board. "As we will be flying over remote areas, this plane is equipped with emergency survival equipment."

The announcement produced another groan from Dietmar.

"You're so neurotic, Oban," Tom laughed.

"It's huge down there," Dietmar said, leaning close to the window. "There's nothing but snow."

Tom wrote some ideas in his notebook. "Here's what I figure," he whispered. "Remember I told you the secret about the hitman?"

"Don't worry, I haven't told anyone."

"I know that, Oban. Now listen up. ZULU-1 wanted to take the micro north to Joe, to hide in a boat. I thought Joe meant a person, but it's the place—Gjoa Haven."

"What use is the micro to anyone?"

"Blackmail! It could prove that the Prime Minister is part of a conspiracy. Dunbar would pay big money to keep that a secret."

"Why take the micro-cassette up north?"

"It's the perfect hiding place. Who'd ever look in Gjoa Haven for the micro?"

"No one except Tom Austen, the defective detective.

You'll waste your entire visit searching for it—and you'll find nothing."

* * *

After serving a delicious lasagna, the flight attendant announced a contest. "Guess the combined age of me and the two pilots, and you can try flying this plane."

"I'll win this," Tom predicted, but he was wrong. Dietmar's guess of 90 years took the prize, and as he went forward, the other students requested permission to leave the plane.

"Fasten your seatbelts," Mr. Plantinga laughed. "We're in for a rough ride."

"I've got to watch this," Tom said, going to the cockpit with his camera. Dietmar sat in the co-pilot's seat, facing the instrument panel. Outside were vistas of endless snow, shadowed by low sunshine from the west.

"It's a white desert," Dietmar said over the droning roar of the engines. "Why aren't there any houses?"

"People live under the snow," the pilot replied. Then he grinned. "Hey, I'm kidding."

"Why no trees?"

"They don't grow this far north."

As the pilot demonstrated the controls, the plane swerved left, producing loud cries from the cabin. The co-pilot laughed. "You're ruining this kid's reputation with his friends."

The pilot pointed to a infinitesimal speck far away in the white landscape. "There's Gjoa, straight ahead. Franklin's men died on that island, Amundsen anchored the *Gjoa* in the harbour, and the Mounties on the *St. Roch* watched these same skies. This is real history, guys!" He grinned at them. "You'll like the people up here. Now, you'd better hustle back to your seats."

In the cabin, the teens with window seats were taking pictures and videos and calling out to their friends as the plane circled before beginning its descent.

"Boy, it's *tiny!*"

"Awesome. We're actually here."

"I'm scared."

"I don't have butterflies in my stomach, I have penguins."

"Look at the sunset!"

Pale shades of cloud covered the sky. The sun glowed red, just above the horizon. "Welcome to Gjoa Haven," said the flight attendant as the wheels bumped down on the frozen land.

Cheers rang out.

The adventure had begun.

WELCOME TO GJOA HAVEN

7

Snow clung to the terminal building, which was the size of a portable classroom. Faces peered through windows, and a welcoming sign in bright colours hung on the wall. When the plane engines stopped, a crowd of people hurried outside, heads down into the wind. They wore heavy-duty parkas with fur-fringed hoods. Their breath blew away in clouds.

As the plane's door opened, the frigid wind rushed in. "Help," Dietmar yelped. "That's brutal!"

"Look," a boy cried, "they've come to the airport on snowmobiles. I want to ride one!"

Outside in the cold wind, the locals and their guests—happily reunited—mingled beside the plane while the luggage was unloaded. Far away across the ivory-coloured snow were the houses of the hamlet's one thousand people.

Junior was among the welcomers; he shook hands with a powerful grip. Faith was also present, clinging to her boyfriend Sam's arm. He no longer had the glasses and scraggly blond beard. But his eyes and nose remained runny.

"Tom," he said, shaking hands. "I'm surprised to see you."

"Austen's crazy," Dietmar said. He was shivering in the cold. "Can you believe it? He dropped out of his tournament to experience *this*."

Sam smiled at Tom. "Good for you."

"I'm excited to be here."

"As for me," Dietmar moaned, "I'll never be warm again."

Sam laughed. "I was like you, my first time north. Scared to death, but then I fell in love with the land and the way of life." He put his arm around Faith. "And with the people."

Constance approached Tom. At her side was the Inuk Mountie. "Good news," Constance said to Tom. "You'll be staying with the Mountie and his family. You can discuss police work together."

Tom enthusiastically shook the man's hand. "Thanks for your hospitality."

He smiled. "Your friend Dietmar Oban will be staying next door at the home of Moses and Rachel. You can visit each other."

"Not if he keeps complaining."

Sam looked at Tom. "I remember your interest in CSIS. You're into crime busting?"

Tom nodded.

"I guess the Mountie has probably mentioned that major crimes don't happen here. This airport is the only exit from town. Escaping would be impossible."

"Except," Junior said, "on the land." He looked at the white landscape that stretched away in all directions. "Out there, a person could hide forever."

* * *

Tom looked at Luke Yates, who was collecting his luggage. "That guy bothers me."

As if reading his mind, Yates snapped his eyes in their direction. Lifting his rifle and a bulky tote bag, he crossed the snow to them. "You're the Mountie here, right?"

"That is correct, sir."

Yates looked around, studying everything. The gum snapped and popped inside his mouth. "I'm here to shoot me an Arctic big white. Where are those polar bears?"

"You must request a hunting tag in advance, sir. You've come a long way for nothing."

Yates studied the Mountie's face. "We're in the middle of nowhere! I don't need a hunting tag up here—I pay my taxes, I've got rights. This trip is costing big bucks, so where are those bears? I'm here to kill one, and I don't need a tag."

"If you hunt illegally, sir, I will arrest you."

Sam gestured at the plane. "First Air is the only exit from Gjoa Haven. They'd never let you fly with an illegal trophy."

Yates looked at the plane, then at Sam and Faith, and then at the Mountie. His jaw moved energetically.

"Okay," he said at last, "I'll buy a hunting tag. How much, Mountie?"

"This year's tags are all taken, sir."

"There's always a way." Yates pulled a wad of bills from his pocket, and peeled off several. "There's gotta be tags around. Get me one."

"Are you attempting to bribe a police officer, sir?"

"Ah, forget it." Yates snapped his fingers at a local parent. "You there! I want somewhere to stay."

"Try the Amundsen Hotel," she replied.

"I don't suppose this dump has a taxi service?"

She pointed at a snow-caked car. "That is our taxi."

Yates started walking toward it, then paused to stare at the Mountie. "I'm here to get me a polar bear, Eskimo. I won't fail."

* * *

Tom was upset by the man's behavior, but wasn't sure what to say. He helped his host carry his gear to a big snowmobile displaying the RCMP crest. As the Mountie roped the luggage on a wooden sled behind, he said, "We call this a *komatik*."

Climbing on the SnowCat behind the Mountie, Tom grabbed tight. "This is great," he yelled, head down against the bitter wind as the powerful machine roared along a frozen road into town. "I can't believe I'm actually in the Arctic!"

Kids were playing hockey in the streets of the hamlet; a lot of snowmobiles buzzed past, but Tom saw no cars and only a single pickup truck. Huskies on chains prowled outside many homes. Power lines were silhouetted against the sky, where a full moon was rising. The snow was blue under the evening light, which shone on the windows and wooden walls of the houses where smoke drifted away from chimneys.

"My office." The Mountie pointed at a small portable building.

Tom looked at an enormous metal tank that rose above the town. "What's that for?"

"Bulk storage for fuel. It holds more than 500,000 litres of gasoline. Barges bring the fuel up the Mackenzie from Hay River."

"That thing could be a target for terrorists. Blow it up, and you'd cause havoc."

"True," the Mountie replied, "but why terrorists in Gjoa Haven?"

Tom pictured the cold eyes of Luke Yates. Maybe not terrorists, he thought to himself, but how about armed thugs? Gjoa would be the perfect hideout for a contract killer.

* * *

At the Mountie's small, cozy house, an excited family was waiting to greet Tom. They watched with grinning faces as he pulled off his parka and boots. "Don't worry about the caribou," the Mountie said, gesturing at a bloody haunch of meat on a chunk of cardboard. "We've got fish and chips waiting for you."

"I wouldn't mind trying some caribou."

"Excellent." Using a small, crescent-shaped knife, the Mountie sliced meat from the haunch for Tom.

"This knife is called an *ulu*. How do you like the caribou, Tom?"

"Not bad," Tom mumbled, forcing himself to swallow the raw meat. "I'll get used to it."

The Mountie led Tom to an elderly woman in a rocking chair; her brown face was creased by wrinkles. After he spoke to her in Inuktitut, she beamed at Tom. "*Qanuritpit.*"

"My mother says, how are you?"

Tom shyly handed her a pin showing Winnipeg's Golden Boy statue. "This is for you, ma'am."

"Aaah!" Eyes glowing, she displayed the pin to the others.

"My mother does not speak English." The Mountie smiled at Tom. "You're a big hit with her. It must be that hair, the colour of flames. It is unusual around here."

Next he introduced his wife and a mob of kids in T-shirts and jeans. "These are not all ours," the Mountie explained. "They are nieces, nephews, cousins, children of cousins. We are one big family in Gjoa Haven."

Digging in his luggage, Tom found the slightly battered pineapple. "Mom sent this."

"Wonderful," the Mountie exclaimed, and the kids whooped with joy. "Fresh fruit is a luxury to us."

Surprised and pleased, Tom pulled apples and oranges from his pack. "Here's more stuff."

"Your parents are kind," the Mountie said. "I enjoyed meeting them."

"They both say hi."

Tom glanced around. A western movie was on TV; it seemed strange to see trees. On the wall above, a poster featured the flashing blades of a hockey great. Outside the window, he saw huskies on chains patrolling their territory; beyond them, the snow went on forever.

"You are looking at the Arctic Ocean, Tom. Your home is straight south of here, more than 2,000 kilometres as the snowy owl flies. The huskies belong to my son, Junior." The Mountie beckoned him to the table. "Now you must eat."

Tom enjoyed a delicious Arctic char with potatoes as the youngest kids stood around the table, staring. "*Teagukpin*?" said the Mountie's mother, offering tea.

The Mountie smiled. "The children call my mother Tea-Granny. She drinks it all day."

"So does my Nan!"

While Tom ate, people kept arriving and leaving. He lost track of the names, but liked all their smiles. Kids ran in and out the front door, yelling in loud voices and rough-housing under people's feet. No one seemed to care.

"We believe that children are the reincarnation of our ancestors," the Mountie explained. "How can I discipline my son if he's really my grandfather?"

His wife nodded. "But do not worry, Tom. The children grow up strong. They have many aunts and uncles, many grandparents. Their wisdom becomes a part of each child."

As Tom helped wash the dishes, he listened to a CB radio crackling out messages. "What's this for?" he asked one of the kids.

"People send messages by CB. Most people in Gjoa have one. Few have telephones."

Junior arrived at the house. After respectfully greeting his grandmother and his parents, Junior chatted with Tom. Then someone knocked loudly on the outside door.

"Must be a *kabloona*," Junior commented. "My people just walk in—we have no secrets."

Several children ran to open the door; in the darkness outside, Tom saw a yellow Ski-Doo. Luke Yates pushed past the kids and advanced on the Mountie, who sat beside his mother watching *Coronation Street* on TV. "Okay, Eskimo—I'll tell you again. I want a hunting tag, and I want it *now*."

The Mountie's mother touched the teapot at her side. "*Teaqukpin*?" she said to Yates.

Ignoring her, Yates leaned over the Mountie. "Some locals have hunting tags, right?" He pointed at a computer in the corner. "The names are in that thing, right? So tell me who they are, and I'll buy a tag from someone."

"I cannot do that, sir. It's against the rules."

Eyes blazing with anger, Yates raised a hand as if to strike the Mountie. Tom expected Junior to defend his father, but the young Inuk didn't do anything.

After a tense moment, Yates lowered his hand, then spat a filthy word in the Mountie's face. Storming out of the house, Yates gave the door a mighty slam.

Junior immediately returned to his conversation with Tom, the soap opera commanded attention once again, and the children returned to their play. It seemed Yates had upset only one person—Tom was enraged.

* * *

"That racist scum," he stormed at Dietmar as they walked around town that night with Moses and Rachel. "I expected Junior to deck him, but he didn't even speak."

Moses nodded. "Junior is a man of strength."

Dietmar laughed. "Strength? You're joking."

Moses didn't react to Dietmar's sarcasm. "My people believe in peaceful coexistence—maybe it comes from living together in igloos. He who attacks another is weak."

"But Yates was so insulting," Tom said.

"All the more reason to show strength. Junior and his father demonstrated their maturity. Luke Yates revealed his weakness."

Although it was nighttime, children rode past on bicycles, giggling as they stared at Tom and Dietmar. A young woman stopped to greet them; on her back was a baby, peeking out from the folds of a brightly decorated packing-parka. The snow crunched underfoot as they continued on to the arena, listening to snowmobiles in the night. "Professor Dunbar was right," Tom said. "The Arctic is the ultimate."

* * *

At the arena, they exchanged smiles with the people of all ages who came in from the cold, wearing beautiful parkas and fur-fringed *kamiks* on their feet. After watching a hockey game, the teens joined the other visitors and their billets in wandering the hamlet under brilliant stars. Tom was warm inside a caribou parka loaned by the Mountie; the *kamiks* he wore on his feet had soles that were slippery on the snowy streets.

For hours, the teens visited house to house, meeting people, talking, staring at everything. Long after midnight, Tom left the home of a friendly boy named Silas Atkichok and crunched through the night, homeward bound.

Ahead loomed the black outline of the bulk storage tank. A wire fence provided security, but its gate stood open. Nearby was a yellow snowmobile that Tom recognized.

He'd seen it earlier when Luke Yates had arrived at the Mountie's house.

* * *

The Ski-Doo's engine was warm. Tom looked at a metal staircase that curved up the side of the tank. Had someone climbed up there?

Sliding silently in his *kamiks* along a frozen path, Tom reached the staircase. He started up, aware of his pounding heart. Somewhere in the night, a dog howled, and others joined in.

Tightly gripping the rail, Tom climbed further. All around were the roofs of houses where people slept peacefully. The cries of the dogs died away, then rose to higher notes. Gulping air, Tom reached the top. A metal catwalk led to the centre of the tank, where someone in a dark parka knelt over large nozzles and other equipment.

The person's head was hidden inside a parka hood. Cautiously, Tom stepped on to the catwalk, hoping for a better view. But his *kamiks* slipped on the icy metal and he suddenly fell sideways.

Tom's hand tore loose from the railing. Landing heavily on the tank's sloped roof, he shouted in horror. His feet couldn't grip, and he was swiftly plunging toward the edge.

8

At the edge of the roof, Tom slammed into a wooden platform. Somehow he seized it, breaking his fall. But his feet went over the side, leaving him dangling in midair.

"Help," Tom yelled.

The person turned toward him, eyes hidden behind snowmobile goggles.

"Please!"

Hurrying along the catwalk, the person disappeared down the staircase. Using all his strength, Tom struggled to safety on the platform and lay gasping in shock. Then, getting to his knees, he crawled along to the staircase. Somewhere below, an engine roared, and moments later the yellow Ski-Doo disappeared into the night.

* * *

The next morning, Tom was awakened by a clock radio. "A cold front is moving along the Arctic coast," said the announcer, "and temperatures will continue to drop. Have a nice day, and be good to yourself."

As she began speaking in Inuktitut, Tom remembered a dream in which he'd played hockey at the Gjoa Haven arena, astounding everyone with his moves. He studied the Canadian flag on the wall above him, then his eyes travelled to a poster of a rock star and a framed award for perfect Sunday school attendance.

Showering under a nozzle shaped like Dracula, Tom thought about the storage tank. He could have died. Shivering, he added hot water. Later, he ate Rice Krispies in bright sunshine while writing in his notebook. Outside the window was the Mountie, feeding Junior's dogs.

After drinking some tea, Tom put on sunglasses and several layers of clothing before stepping into air so icy that it pinched his nostrils painfully. The Mountie's face beamed a greeting from inside his parka. "*Ublaqut*, Tom Austen. This means good morning."

"*Ub . . . la . . . qut*," Tom replied, struggling with the word.

"*Hila unaituq*. It is cold."

After hearing Tom's description of the events at the fuel storage depot, the Mountie promised to investigate immediately. Tom offered to help, but was politely reminded of the morning's special assembly at the school. "The mayor will welcome your class. You are special guests in our community."

"You're right. It's important that we all be present."

Tom eyed the huskies. They were securely chained, but he still kept his distance. Beyond them was the frozen sea; tiny diamonds of light reflected from the bright snow.

"It's beautiful here."

"Thank you." The Mountie looked toward the west. "Long ago, our ancestors came from Asia. This is a splendid place they found." He tapped the snow with his foot. "On this land, my grandparents walked, and their grandparents before them. It has long been so."

The Mountie and Tom returned to the front door, where they said goodbye. Dietmar was just leaving with the twins from their house, and Tom joined them.

"*Ublaqut*," he said. "*Hila unaituq.*"

Rachel grinned. "Very good, Tom."

As they climbed a frozen slope, Dietmar yawned. "I've been awake for 37 hours straight, playing Nintendo and hanging out. The sunrise was cool to see, but I didn't eat breakfast. It was raw caribou."

Moses smiled. "Wait until we have ptarmigan heart, Dietmar. It is good and soft."

"Yech."

Reaching the top of the hill, they passed the bulk storage tank. True to his word, the Mountie had arrived to investigate, and waved to them from the metal stairs. A lot of kids and parents were walking through town toward the school, which was a large building painted a brilliant orange.

In the twins' classroom, they peeled off their outer clothing. The technology was typical of any well-equipped school, but the posters were unique, showing snow-swept vistas and the faces of northern celebrities like the singing star Susan Aglukark and her Arctic Rose Band.

In the hallway, posters gave instructions on building an igloo. "Look at the exit sign," said Adam Marx, joining them for the walk to the gym. "It's in their language. That's cool."

A large crowd had gathered in the gym. Students of all ages sat on the floor; seated around the walls were grandparents, parents, and babies. After the singing of *O Canada* in English and Inuktitut, a prayer was given. Then the mayor stepped to the microphone with words of welcome; he was young and wore jeans and a "Screaming Eagles" sweatshirt. As the visitors were introduced and gifts were exchanged, many people recorded the event on video, including Rachel and Moses, who had twin Sonys.

The assembly ended with a display of Arctic Games. "When our people lived on the land," the mayor explained, "we would gather in a *qaggi*, a large snow house where singing and games took place. Today, people from the polar nations gather every two years for Arctic Games to test our skills and renew friendships."

The school's gym teacher demonstrated the Alaska high kick. A bit of cloth was hung from the basketball hoop; with a mighty leap, he managed to kick the cloth and then land in the same precise spot. Huge applause rang out.

"That's amazing," Adam exclaimed.

"You should try it," Moses suggested.

"No, thanks!"

The teacher called for volunteers to attempt the knuckle-hop. "It's like doing push-ups, only on your knuckles and toes. You have to hop forward—our school record is one lap of the gym."

As the southern teens whimpered at the thought, Tom was astonished to see Dietmar raise his hand. "I'll try."

He managed to knuckle-hop for several metres before collapsing. As cheers broke out, Dietmar waved to the crowd and grinned. "That was fun," he exclaimed, returning to sit with the others.

"I'm impressed," Tom admitted.

Next, they toured the town. The first stop was the Northern store, where everything possible was for sale, from snowmobiles to CDs to frozen pizza. When the friendly manager showed them the storage area, they discovered pop in huge stacks that reached to the ceiling.

"Every summer, a barge arrives with a year's supply of this stuff." The manager smiled. "Folks here love soft drinks—maybe it's the caffeine."

Lots of people were in the store. Tom posed Dietmar and the twins against a display of northern clothes, then took a close-up of a solemn-eyed toddler in furs.

"Things are expensive here," Dietmar said, as they left the store.

Moses nodded. "Prices are 82 percent higher than in Yellowknife."

"Yet another reason," Dietmar said, "to avoid this place in future."

Mr. Cousins approached them. "Tom, someone just contacted me from the hotel. A fax has arrived for you."

"Hey," Tom exclaimed. "This could be from Dad, about the murders. Can I go get it, sir?"

"Sure. Our next stop is the town hall, for a visit with the mayor. Catch up with us there."

Rachel decided to accompany Tom. He took photos as they crunched along the snow-packed streets in their *kamiks*. "Sorry about Dietmar's sarcasm," Tom said to Rachel. "I hope you're not upset."

"Thanks, Tom, but I don't mind what Dietmar says. I understand him. He is an unhappy person."

"Yeah, it's true. His home life isn't much fun."

Dietmar came running to join them. "Let's have a hot chocolate at the hotel, okay?" He smiled at Rachel. "I'm buying."

The Amundsen was a small, single-storey building. Quite a few snowmobiles were parked outside; some were yellow, and had the words *Amundsen Hotel* on them.

Inside, Sam was working at a desk. On it, a large photograph of Faith was displayed in a silver frame. "I'm the hotel manager," he explained to Tom. "This fax arrived for you."

Quickly, Tom read it. "It's not about the murders. Liz wants me to find a carving for Zoltan's birthday."

"That's her boyfriend?" Rachel asked.

Tom nodded.

"Let's get that hot chocolate," Dietmar said.

They went into the small dining room. It was smoky, and filled with people. "Government workers," Rachel said, "on a coffee break."

Tom saw Faith and Junior together at an arborite

table. She was speaking urgently and gesturing. "Are they civil servants?"

Rachel shook her head. "Faith and Junior own a business together. At night, they clean the town hall and places like that."

"Sam's eyes looked bad today," Tom commented. "He says it's an allergy, but I wonder . . . "

"Yes?"

"Look at Faith and Junior—that's an intense conversation they're having. Maybe Sam's love life is a mess, and he's been crying."

"I doubt it," Rachel said. "Junior would never betray Sam. They're close friends."

Tom shrugged. "Stranger things have happened."

The only available seats were at a table with Luke Yates. The writer smelled of a strong aftershave; he was staring moodily at the arborite. Tom remembered the storage tank, and his skin prickled. The man could not be trusted.

Luke Yates looked at Rachel. "Anyone in your family a hunter?"

"Yes."

"Great! Have they got a polar bear tag? I'll pay good money."

"We do not hunt polar bear," Rachel replied. "There is no such tag in my house."

Luke Yates swore, and angrily slapped the table. "I'll find one!"

Tom sipped the hot chocolate provided by Dietmar. "Thanks, Oban." He looked at Yates. "Why kill a polar bear? What's the big deal?"

"It's one of the supreme trophies," Yates explained.

"Like a Siberian tiger, or a grizzly. Bag one of those, and you're acknowledged as a champion hunter."

"Aren't they endangered species?"

Luke Yates shook his head in disgust. "What's wrong with kids these days? All that garbage about animal rights—are you sick in the head, or what?"

Tom felt his skin glowing. "What about you," he said, struggling to control his temper. "What's wrong with *you*, killing defenceless animals! The government should take away your rifle."

Yates laughed. "That'll never happen. Especially when the referendum passes, and we join the United States. Down there, the gun laws make sense. It's written in their constitution—people have the right to bear arms. Once we're part of the States, I'll have that right, too. I'm thinking of opening a store in Winnipeg to sell handguns and ammo. The money will be good—every house will need weapons for self-defense." He stared at his coffee cup. "I'm sick of being a freelance writer. I'm good, but it's still hard to scratch up enough stories to make a buck."

Dietmar grinned at Rachel. "Austen's been talking recently about becoming a writer some day. That's as unrealistic as being a detective."

Luke Yates chuckled. "A kid detective, huh? Had any luck?"

"A bit," Tom replied.

Dietmar grinned. "Tell him your latest theory, Austen. About the hitman being loose in Gjoa Haven."

Tom groaned. "You fool, Oban! That's confidential information."

Luke Yates narrowed his eyes. "A contract killer, *here*? Give me the details."

Tom was saved from replying when Sam spoke. He'd been standing by the table, listening to the conversation. "There's a phone call for you, Mr. Yates. It sounds important."

"Stay here," Yates warned Tom. "I've got questions to ask you."

As he walked away, Sam sat down. "Was that guy bothering you?" he asked Rachel.

She shook her head.

Within a minute, Yates was back. "There wasn't a phone call." He gave Sam a dirty look, then glanced across the noisy room at Faith and Junior. "That's your girlfriend, right? Well, mister, take my advice. Never trust an Eskimo."

"I've got a suggestion to make," Sam said to Yates. "Catch the next flight out. You won't find a hunting tag in Gjoa, and you're just causing trouble. If you continue to insult the Inuit, I'll throw you out of this hotel."

"I'm not a quitter, mister. When I want something, I get it." Yates pointed a finger at Tom. "I'll speak to you later."

As the writer walked out of the dining room, Sam shook his head. "What a loser," he sighed. "That guy actually believes the Inuit created all their problems, when in fact they lived in absolute balance with their world before the first *kabloonas* arrived and started killing everything in sight. We took away these people's rights, laughed at their traditions, herded them into settlements. What happened was a tragedy."

Changing the subject, Sam asked, "You enjoyed the assembly at school?"

"You bet," Dietmar said.

"I loved the Arctic Games," Tom said. "Can that teacher ever jump!"

"He's called Laser because of his volleyball serve. Don't get in front of it!" Sam waved at Faith and Junior. "Come join us."

As the pair crossed the dining room, Tom noticed Faith dabbing at her eyes with a Kleenex. She gave Junior an unhappy smile before sitting down.

"More trouble with that guy Yates?" Junior asked Sam.

"Yes. I keep hoping he'll go home to Winnipeg."

"I have a hunting tag," Junior said, "but that *kabloona* won't get it."

Sam turned to Faith. "We were discussing the Arctic Games, honey." He smiled proudly at the others. "Faith's a world champion. She took a gold and two bronzes at the last games in Alaska. The medals are shaped like *ulu* knives."

"Congratulations," Dietmar said. "I've had some experience with those games. They're brutal."

She smiled shyly. "The medals are not important. It is the sense of family, the unity of the people. We cheer all competitors, and help each other. To be there makes me happy." She looked at Sam. "You should tell them about your high school golds."

"I was pretty good with the javelin," Sam told them. "But sports down south are too competitive for me. Up here, nobody is made to feel like a loser."

"Guess what?" Tom said. "The Mountie is planning

a trip out on the land for me. I can hardly wait! The other Mountie gets back from holidays on Sunday, so we're leaving right away. We'll overnight at the ice-fishing igloo, then push on to the Franklin Cairn and maybe Starvation Cove. Have you ever seen the cairn?"

Sam nodded. "It's just a pile of rocks with a small sign, but it's real history. That's where long-ago explorers found some bones and skulls of sailors from the Franklin expedition."

"Wow! I bet there are ghosts everywhere!"

Sam smiled. Then he turned to Faith, and asked about her family. As they spoke, Junior stood up and quickly walked away. He didn't say goodbye.

* * *

When they rejoined the others, the tour was just leaving the town hall. "They've got a small museum in there," Mr. Cousins reported. "It's worth seeing."

Through his sunglasses, Tom watched some little kids in parkas building a small igloo, while others played with dolls and toy trucks. Then he saw a yellow snowmobile approaching, and his heart beat rapidly. Was it Luke Yates, looking for trouble?

Faith was on the machine. "Tom," she said, "you're wanted back at the hotel."

"Another fax?"

Faith shook her head. "Jump on fast, okay? It's important."

Mr. Plantinga checked their schedule. "Meet us at the Coop, Tom. We're seeing a demonstration of carving."

Tom climbed on behind Faith, and the yellow snow-mobile buzzed quickly through town to the Amundsen. Sam was behind the desk. "Thanks for coming, Tom." He looked at Faith. "Would you run things for five minutes, sweetheart?"

In the hotel office, Sam motioned Tom into a chair and sat on the edge of the desk. "Tom, I've just spoken to your father at Winnipeg police HQ."

"Hey! Is there a break in the murder investigation?"

"It looks possible." Taking out his wallet, Sam handed Tom a white business card. In one corner was the Canadian flag, with the initials CSIS underneath. Printed in black letters was the name *Samuel G. White*.

Tom's eyes bulged in surprise. "You're with CSIS?"

Sam nodded. "Working at this hotel is a cover. My territory covers the entire western Arctic."

"Remember when we talked at the James Bay Inn? No wonder you knew about CSIS!"

Sam nodded. "I went to Winnipeg on an agency matter. My disguise included the beard and eyeglasses." He smiled briefly, then became serious. "I just called your father on a secure line. I asked his permission to tell you I'm CSIS, Tom, because your theory is absolutely right. Like you, we believe ZULU-1 is in Gjoa Haven."

9

For a moment, Tom was speechless. Then he said, "How can I help?"

"First, tell me who you suspect."

"Luke Yates."

Sam nodded. "That's not a surprise. Why him?"

"Yates has a rifle, so he understands weapons. He was nearby at the time of both murders and, in fact, I saw Yates outside the professor's office just before the shooting."

"Anything else?"

Tom described the events at the storage tank. "I'm sure Yates was responsible."

Sam wrote some notes. "I'll keep your Dad advised of developments, using the secure line. If you're phoning home, Tom, don't say *one word* about this. Anyone in town can listen to long distance calls being radioed south."

"I understand," Tom replied. "What about the Mountie—should I tell him about Yates?"

Sam shook his head. "Gjoa Haven is deep cover for me. Even the Mountie doesn't know the truth." He stood up. "I'll have my people in Ottawa check on Luke Yates. I'll advise you what we learn, and what action is planned." He shook Tom's hand. "Good work."

"Thanks! I hope something really exciting happens while I'm in Gjoa."

"Maybe it will."

* * *

Later that day, Tom decided to catch some of the annual Hamlet Days events. At the snow-packed harbour he saw a small boat which had been abandoned for the winter and hurried to it, remembering that the microcassette could be hidden in a boat. But drifting snow had filled the motorboat to the gunnels; it would be impossible to search.

A yellow Safari roared to a stop beside Tom. Faith was at the controls. "Want to try this thing, Tom?"

"You bet!"

Soon they were moving fast, cutting figure eights into the snow. Finally, Tom stopped the machine near the crowd that had gathered for the special events. "Thanks," he said with a grin at Faith, as they stepped off the machine.

"No problem."

The Mountie was there, and he smiled at Tom. "I

have investigated the storage tanks. Nothing was tampered with, but the lock on the gate was picked by an expert."

"Thanks for letting me know." Tom looked across the harbour. "That big boat over there, with the cabin. What's its name?"

"*Netsilik*. It means seal."

"Okay to look inside?"

"I'm sure that would be fine. Any reason?"

Tom shrugged. "Just curiosity," he replied, feeling guilty about avoiding the question. As the Mountie began talking to someone else, Tom crossed the snow to the Ladies' Igloo-Building event. One of the competitors was Faith, and Sam was present to cheer her on.

Racing against the clock, each woman quickly traced the outline of an igloo and then began cutting large blocks of snow using *panas*, long knives that glittered in the sunlight. As the crowd rooted them on and video cameras rolled, the women lifted the blocks into place. Quickly the walls grew.

"I can't believe how fast they're working," Tom said to Sam, "and look at *that* woman go. She must be 80 years old!"

"Last year Elsie won with a time of 22 minutes," Sam replied, "and I think she's about to repeat her victory."

The woman dropped the last block into place, quickly smoothed the snow with her *pana*, then raised both hands and grinned as the audience cheered her success. Moments later, the Mountie's wife finished her snow house, followed by Faith. All three congratulated each other.

Sam hugged Faith as she joined them, gasping for air. Sweat poured down her face. "That Elsie, she's so good."

"What's next, honey?" Sam asked.

"The harpoon throw."

"No problem—that's your gold medal event from Fairbanks."

Tom crawled into Faith's igloo. It was beautiful inside, filled with an ethereal light. From the entrance, he took a picture of the full moon far above in the blue sky, and then he wriggled out. "I can't believe I'm in this amazing place," he exclaimed to Faith as he lined up a shot of the snow-swept harbour. "I keep thinking about Amundsen arriving here, or those Mounties in the *St. Roch*. Imagine—they were at this very spot."

Using Faith's *pana*, Tom began constructing an igloo. Within moments he was sweating hard, and he quit after making one crooked snow block. "I'm not cut out for this work," he joked to the others.

"Long ago," Sam said, "the *pana* was made from a caribou antler. Imagine cutting snow blocks with that." He wiped his runny nose. "They made enormous igloos back then, as large as 20 feet in diameter. Imagine sleeping on a bed made of snow! When their homes melted in the spring, people moved into tents."

Tom photographed a mother and her child affectionately brushing their faces together. After herding together the local teens and their visitors for a picture, he captured Dietmar on film with the twins. All three were very cheerful. "Look at this carving Moses gave me," Dietmar said. In his hand was an Inuk with a husky, carved from ivory. "This guy is living free.

Look at his happiness. Know what's nice here? People smile at you in the street, and they ask questions. They actually *care* about you. It's so amazing."

"You're getting to like this place," Tom said.

Dietmar nodded. "I phoned my Mom to say I love it here. She started crying, I don't know why."

"Because," Rachel said, smiling, "she's happy for you."

"Wasn't that igloo-building event something else?" Tom said.

Moses looked proudly at his sister. "Rachel is entered in the same event for teens. She's really good, but Sheena Kamookak is tops."

Faith looked across the harbour. Sam followed her eyes, and then frowned. The yipping and yapping of a dog team announced the arrival of Junior, cracking a long whip in the air. The huskies were magnificent, straining against their leads as steam rushed from their mouths and nostrils.

Junior grinned at the crowd. "You kids from the south," he called. "Who wants a dog team ride?"

Dietmar quickly raised his hand to volunteer, and bumped away on a *komatik* behind Junior and the team. There was a big smile on his face.

Sam left for the hotel. Tom was getting cold, but he stayed for Faith's final event. She was a champion at throwing the harpoon—a long pole with a sharpened point—and he wanted to watch.

"What an arm," he exclaimed, after Faith success-fully took the event. "Congratulations."

"Thank you," she said. Then the happiness faded from Faith's face. Coming across the frozen harbour was Luke Yates on a yellow snowmobile. "That guy," she said. "He is trouble."

"You bet he is," Tom agreed. "In fact, Yates could easily be . . . "

Tom slammed his mouth shut. *Fool* he thought to himself—maybe Faith didn't know about Sam's link to CSIS. He'd almost released confidential information!

Faith's beautiful eyes were studying his face. "Yates could possibly be what?"

"Nothing," Tom mumbled.

Faith said nothing more. They both watched Luke Yates walking through the crowd, talking to people and waving around a wad of money. "He's desperate for a hunting tag," Tom remarked.

"He won't get one," Faith said.

Luke Yates approached them. "Listen, kid, what about that contract killer? Give me some information, okay? I could sell that story, and make big money. I'll give you a cut."

"No comment," Tom replied.

Faith said nothing. Her eyes darted between their faces.

Yates studied Tom through narrow eyes. "If you change your mind, contact me at the Amundsen. I'm offering good money."

Climbing on the snowmobile, he roared across the harbour. "He's heading for the *Netsilik*," Tom said. "Listen, Faith, may I borrow your Safari?"

"Sure thing."

Powering up the machine, Tom followed Luke Yates at a safe distance. He thought the man might be planning to hide something in the *Netsilik*, but Yates passed the snowed-in boat without stopping. Roaring up a hill, the yellow snowmobile disappeared over the crest.

Tom slowed his machine, and glanced back at the distant crowd. Hoping Faith didn't need her Safari in a hurry, he continued up the hill.

From the crest, Tom saw Luke Yates in the distance. He was travelling fast, heading away from town. Staying a good distance behind, Tom followed Yates until he reached the dump.

Leaving his snowmobile in hiding, Tom crept to the top of a hill. Using his binoculars, he watched Yates stare at the snow-covered mounds of rubbish. For a long time the man stood without moving; then he seemed to make a decision.

Yates walked to an abandoned snowmobile. The windshield was missing, and it was thick with snow. Suddenly Yates bent forward. His body blocked Tom's view but he seemed to reach for something, then put it inside his parka. After that, the man walked rapidly back to his snowmobile.

With a big smile on his face, Luke Yates headed for town.

* * *

Tom roared back to the harbour, where events were wrapping up. "Sorry I took off with your machine," he said to Faith.

"You followed that guy?"

Tom nodded.

"Why?"

Tom avoided Faith's eyes. "It was just—something to do."

Saying goodbye, Tom hurried to the hotel. Inside the dining room, Sam was sitting alone with a coffee. Joining him, Tom described the mysterious trip to the dump by Luke Yates.

Sam listened intently. "That's really valuable information." He stood up. "I'll check it out immediately. Excellent work, Tom!"

Glowing with pleasure, Tom walked home with the snow squeaking underfoot. When the Mountie returned, Tom went outside with him to feed Junior's dogs. The air was intensely cold. The snow was blue, and so was the sky. The sun was small in the west, glowing with an orange light.

Seeing their food approach, the huskies pawed the snow and strained against their long leads. Their ears pointed forward, their bushy tails straight up. "Each has a personality," the Mountie said, tossing frozen char to the huskies, who snatched it from the air. "Aqnaq is a hard worker. Kajuq is playful and Kumaq is lovable, but they are not good pullers."

The food was gone within moments. "I'm very happy here," Tom said, photographing the huskies from a safe distance.

"You are a welcome guest, Tom. Ah, here is my son."

Junior had approached from behind, moving silently. Tom was startled by his sudden appearance, but managed a smile. "*Qanuritpit*, Junior. *Hila unaituq*."

"It sure is cold! In February, we hit 80 below with the wind chill. I was alone on the land, but I survived. I love it out there."

"Do people ever get lost?"

"Many have died, Tom. Inuit, and people from elsewhere. One recent summer, three students from Japan drowned during a canoe expedition. The people of Cambridge Bay warned them of an approaching storm, but they journeyed on. Nothing was found except a Seiko watch on a severed arm."

"Wow—I'll put that in my notebook for sure. Have you ever seen a polar bear?"

"Yes. I have hunted them."

"That doesn't seem right."

"This land is our farm," Junior replied. "It is how we feed our people. You've seen the price of food from the south? After I kill an animal, I kneel to thank it, for the gift of nourishment. I pour water in the animal's mouth, to ease its journey to the spirit world."

The Mountie nodded solemnly. "Some of our hunters sell their game, to buy food for their families. These days, unhappily, people in Europe refuse to purchase anything that has been hunted. As a result, many people are hungry."

"We do not kill for trophies," Junior said quietly. "It would be against our beliefs."

"That guy Yates bugs me," Tom said. "I'm glad he hasn't found a polar bear tag."

"I've got one," Junior said, "but he can't have it."

The Mountie looked at his son with worried eyes. "Be cautious around that man. He carries evil in his soul."

"Don't worry, Father. He will not harm me."

* * *

After a supper of delicious Arctic char, radio bingo was played by those in the community who had CBs. Tom listened to the game for a while, then picked up the family scrapbook and flipped through it. One part was devoted to Junior's career in the army, where his unit had received special training on bomb disposal and demolitions. Tom also saw several pictures of Faith and Junior together.

Later in the evening, he was alone in the house when the CB radio spluttered out his name. *Tom Austen*, said a man's voice. *Report to the arena immediately*.

Surprised, Tom stared at the radio, but the message wasn't repeated. After a moment's thought, he wrote on a piece of paper ARTICLES RENTED ENDLESSLY NEVER ARRIVE. "That's good backup," he said to himself, leaving the note on the table, "just in case I don't return. Rachel will figure it out."

Outside, Tom covered his cheeks and nose with his caribou mitts, worried about frostbite. The moon was huge in the black sky as he walked quickly through the bitter cold until he saw the arena ahead.

Lots of people were inside, watching fast-paced hockey. Tom walked slowly around, searching the faces. Had the message come from Sam? There was no sign of him, or Faith.

During a break in the hockey action, a woman's voice announced over the loudspeakers, "Message for Tom Austen at the concession stand."

When Tom reached the stand, he was handed an envelope. "This just arrived for you," said the friendly woman behind the counter.

Amundsen Hotel was printed in a corner of the envelope. "Who brought this?" Tom asked, tearing it open.

"The taxi driver. Someone paid him to drive it over."

Inside the envelope was a slip of paper. On it were the words, *Report to the cemetery. Tell no one.*

Quickly, Tom scribbled a note that read CALIFORNIA ELEPHANTS MEMORIZE ENTIRE TUNES ENDLESSLY ROWING YACHTS. "Please keep this," he asked the woman behind the counter. "Just in case I disappear."

She smiled. "Nobody disappears in Gjoa. This isn't the big city, like on TV."

Tom waved goodbye to her, and stepped into the empty night.

* * *

Burrowed down in his caribou parka, Tom walked resolutely toward the cemetery. His heart thumped heavily. Above, the black sky was lustrous with stars, but Tom couldn't pay attention. Who had sent the messages?

The cemetery was in the middle of town, near the huge fuel storage tank. A large white cross was surrounded by snow. In its shadow was a man. He waved Tom forward. It was Luke Yates.

The writer's head was bare, and his coat was open at the throat. "Thanks for coming, kid. I don't want anyone to know about this meeting—that's why the messages."

Tom kept his distance from Yates. "What's going on?"

"First, tell me about the hit man. Who's your suspect?"

Tom stepped back a pace, ready to leave. "I can't tell you anything about that. Sorry."

"I'll give you cash, up front." Yates patted his pocket. "I've got plenty."

Tom turned to go. "No, thanks."

"Wait, kid!" Yates stepped forward, out of the shadow of the cross. "One more thing, and for this I'm offering *real* money. Break into the Mountie's computer, and get me the names of people in town with a polar bear tag."

"Not a chance."

Yates pulled money out of his pocket. "Everyone's greedy," he said. "Here, take some."

Tom walked away. His back felt vulnerable, but instead of bullets, Luke Yates hurled insults. "You stupid little creep. Here's your chance, get some money! Stop playing the hero, you're just a nothing."

Rachel came running out of the night. "Tom! Are you okay?"

"Sure," he replied. "I'm fine."

From the cemetery, Luke Yates yelled, "Eskimo lover!"

"What's his problem?" Rachel asked.

"He just failed to bribe me." As they began walking home, Tom smiled. "You figured out my messages?"

"Sure—it was easy. I dropped by the Mountie's to say hi, and found your code. But what's going on?"

Tom could only shrug his shoulders and say, "Nothing much." He longed to discuss the case with Rachel, but he was sworn to secrecy. He could tell no one that a contract killer might be in Gjoa Haven, ready to strike again.

10

The next morning, Tom was awake early. The class would be overnighting in igloos, and he was both excited and apprehensive.

The students gathered outside the school with their gear. Everyone was dressed for ultimate cold. "Guess what I'm wearing," Rebecca Bowden said to Tom. "Three pairs of socks, caribou socks, liners, *kamiks*, tights, jeans, snowpants, caribou pants, T-shirt, flannel pj top, sweater, parka, caribou parka, gloves, caribou mitts, scarf, and sunglasses. And I am extremely, extremely hot."

Moses approached with his arm around Dietmar's shoulders. "Your buddy is becoming a real Inuk. Last night, he ate raw caribou with our family."

"It was okay stuff," Dietmar told Tom, "much

better than that earthworm soup you served me in the Kootenays."

"That was just mushroom soup."

"So you claim, Austen, but I'll never believe you."

The teens helped the adults pack their gear on *komatiks* covered with caribou skins, then climbed on for the ride. Towed by snowmobiles, the big sleds bumped through town and entered the wilderness. The sky was clear above the frozen sea, with a yellow sun small in the south. Tom wore wolf-skin mitts against the wind, and thick wool across his face.

"This land is a good one," Moses said, as the caravan picked up speed.

"It sure is big," Tom replied, watching the sunlight reflect from a circle of ice. His teeth rattled together each time the *komatik* slammed over another wind-formed ridge.

"You could travel from here to Asia," Moses said, "and never cross a road."

"That would be a lonely journey."

"Junior loves it out here. This is his natural home, I think, far from anyone."

Eventually, they were waved to a stop by the leader of the expedition. "He has seen something," Moses whispered. "Look, there! Musk-oxen. We call them *oominqmaq*, meaning the animal with skin like a beard."

Their big bodies were covered with brown fur. Tom counted six adults, protectively encircling a young calf. The musk-oxen raised their shaggy heads to study the intruders, then suddenly broke and ran. Clouds of snow swirled from their hooves.

"Wow," Tom exclaimed. "Seeing them makes me feel like a time traveller! Musk-oxen have lived here *forever*."

As Tom put away his camera, Moses smiled. "You'll have lots of pictures of *oominqmaq*. I stopped counting after the first ten."

"I guess I got carried away."

Although Tom hoped to see a polar bear, they encountered no more animals on the journey to the igloos that had been constructed at the ice-fishing site. Groaning, Tom stood up from the *komatik*. "What a ride—I ache all over." Grabbing his gear, he dragged it into the nearest igloo. Light seeped between the blocks, shining on the snow where he would sleep that night.

Tom touched the chocolate bar in his pack, looking forward to a treat. Outside the igloo, he and the others kept warm by rolling down a hill and then playing Arctic Games. Someone found a harpoon inside an igloo, and they tried tossing it. "Are these permanent igloos?" Tom asked Moses.

He nodded. "There are supplies left here, for travellers, and a short-wave radio in case anyone needs help. I'll show you."

An aerial dangled from a pole near the biggest igloo. Inside, the radio crackled and spluttered. "There's another radio at the Amundsen Hotel," Moses explained.

They rode snowmobiles and played soccer and tried ice fishing, but caught only ice. When Tom unwrapped his chocolate bar, it was frozen, but he still ate it. He was very hungry. As the sky grew dark, the wind picked up, driving some people into igloos while others continued to play in the snow.

Finally, Tom went inside. Warmth came from a Cole-man stove, which was vented through a small opening in the domed roof. He sat down, warming his hands. "I'm learning so much in the Arctic. I'll never be the same."

"Promises, promises," Dietmar responded.

"You know something amazing? The pattern of each snowflake is unique—no two are the same."

"Prove it."

Moses grinned. "You two are a laugh."

"Listen to the wind," Tom said, tilting his head.

An elder taught them a traditional string game called *ayarak*, then prepared musk-oxen stew on the stove. "It tastes like steak," Mr. Plantinga said, when the food was served. "You kids eat up, okay? Your bodies burn a lot of energy keeping warm."

"I'm glad I've eaten musk-oxen," Desmond Chan commented, "just to say I did." They celebrated his birthday with a frozen cake, then went outside to play under the stars. The igloos glowed with light, beautiful in the darkness.

Tom walked a short distance into the wilderness, and stood looking at the radiant stars. He was at peace with the world.

* * *

In the middle of the night, Tom awoke. The stove was out, and his toque had fallen off. His hair had frozen! For a moment, this seemed important, and then he drifted back into a dream in which a polar bear bounded across the dark night, pursued by Luke Yates. Tom stirred in his sleep, murmuring in fear.

With morning came the smell of tea brewing. Someone had put frozen pop beside the stove to thaw, but the bottle had exploded and pop was now frozen across the wall. Tom went outside to the biffy—a separate small igloo—and then hurried back for a breakfast of oatmeal and Mr. Noodles.

After breaking camp, they headed for Gjoa Haven. As the *komatik* bumped along the streets to the school, Tom felt good. "The sled dog race is this afternoon," Rachel said. "Come with us, okay?"

After agreeing on a time to meet, Tom hurried to the hotel. Fortunately, Sam wasn't busy and had time to talk. "I've had some feedback from CSIS headquarters," he told Tom. "Luke Yates has a criminal record for violence. We're doing further checks, and I'm expecting an arrest very soon."

"Excellent," Tom exclaimed. "Listen, have you talked to Dad lately?"

"I spoke to your parents an hour ago. They miss you, and send their love. Liz was still asleep—she went dancing last night with someone named Zoltan. Is that her boyfriend?"

Tom nodded.

"Anyway," Sam continued, "there's interesting news. Your Mom will be flying to Ottawa to join a television panel. A group of citizens will be debating U-SAC with the Prime Minister."

"Great!"

Sam handed him a daily newspaper from Edmonton. "This arrived on today's plane. The debate is a big story across the country." Photos of the panel members were on the front page. Tom's mother looked wonderful, and he glowed with pride. "The newspaper says the debate is tomorrow. I can't wait."

Tom described the meeting at the cemetery. "Yates is a weird guy."

Sam nodded. "Therefore, Tom, keep clear of him. Your parents say you're adventurous and a risk-taker. Not on my turf, okay?"

"Sure," Tom said, disappointed. "I understand. This is a matter for professionals, right? Amateurs need not apply."

"Don't be blue," Sam said, smiling. "Tell you what—the moment something breaks, I'll contact you. Maybe I'll need help in some way."

"Fabulous! That would be great."

* * *

Back at the house, Tom ate lunch while telling the family about his trip on the land. Then he left for the dog team races. "I hear Junior's a competitor," he called from the door to the Mountie's wife. "I'll be cheering for him!"

She waved goodbye from the kitchen window as Tom walked toward the ice with Dietmar and the twins. Dogs were howling all over town. "They're lonely," Moses explained. "Only the best pullers are chosen for the race. The others stay home."

"It's already started?"

"The teams left two hours ago. They travel out eleven kilometers, then head back to Gjoa."

"I'd get lost. There aren't any highway signs."

"Or billboards," Dietmar laughed.

"I see Luke Yates—I wonder why he's here?"

A crowd of all ages had arrived by snowmobile and on foot. The sunny air was festive with laughter and the sound of children playing. The only sullen face belonged to Yates, who sat on a yellow Ski-Doo away from everyone. In the distance, at the top of the hill, the fuel storage tank dominated the community. Tom photographed a boy playing with his husky pup, then chatted with the local teachers.

"The women raced this morning," Frieda said, "and there was a big crowd to cheer them home. People here celebrate each other so wonderfully."

"I'm glad you think so." Laser, the gym teacher, smiled. "I hope you and Constance will stay forever in our community."

"I certainly will," Constance replied. She bounced a baby in her arms; her husband, a handsome Inuk, was shooting the scene with his video camera. "This little fellow would miss his extended family."

"Everyone here has such respect for the elders," Tom said. "I like that."

"The old have overcome many difficulties," Laser commented. "Their wisdom helps us all."

A shout went up, and faces turned to the horizon. Clapping began as a tiny speck grew into an approaching shape, and then became a figure in a caribou parka urging on his dogs. "It's Junior," Moses cried. "Come on!"

The excited crowd ran forward to surround the victor. Junior was lifted high on his *komatik* as people cheered. Then he ran with the crowd to greet the next sled.

As Tom photographed Junior's huskies rolling in

the snow, he saw Luke Yates climb off the Ski-Doo. Approaching Junior, Yates pointed a finger in the other man's face. "I just found out. You've got a hunting tag. I want it."

"My tag is not for sale."

The crowd fell silent. Yates stepped closer to Junior. "*I want that tag*. Turn it over, or there'll be big trouble. For you—and your family. Got that?"

Junior said nothing.

"Say something," Yates yelled. "You stupid Eskimo!"

When Junior remained silent, Yates stormed to the Ski-Doo and powered it up. "I won't forget you," he shouted at Junior.

Tom watched the snowmobile roar away. "I wish that guy would leave town."

"He's an ugly *kabloona* for sure," Frieda observed. "I think he's a secret boozer. I smelled alcohol when he was shopping at the Northern."

"Junior's a big guy—I thought he'd plant a fist on Yates. Anyone else would have lost it by now."

"No chance," Laser said. "My people value emotional control. It's the ultimate maturity."

* * *

"Junior will snap eventually," Tom predicted, as he walked home later with Rachel.

"Know what happened in Winnipeg?" she said. "Those guys happened to be shopping in the same store, and Yates told the manager Junior was a shoplifter. Junior was kicked out."

"What a creep."

For hours Tom simmered, thinking about Luke Yates's cruelty. He was still troubled as he walked to the community hall that night with his friends. The black air was crisp; kids played outside on their bikes, and snowmobiles buzzed past.

"It's so cold tonight," Dietmar said. "Even the marrow of my bones is frozen."

Moses laughed. "Is that why you're holding hands with my sister? To keep warm?"

Outside the community hall, they talked to Junior, who'd arrived on a yellow Safari. "This is Faith's machine," he explained, "but she's busy tonight." Inside, people sat facing a large floor. All ages were present for the drum dance in honour of the visitors. People in parkas and jeans sat around the walls, many holding babies; children chased each other everywhere.

Tom and his friends found chairs beside the teachers. In front of them, an older man in a baseball cap and parka was circling while pounding a large drum. On the stage, a woman chanted a song in Inuktitut.

Laser leaned toward Tom. "My people have always celebrated with feasts and drum dancing. It was our entertainment. These days, sadly, video games and satellite TV amuse the young. Few of them dance with the drum."

Finished, the old man walked to Tom and offered him the drum. Tom's face flared red; everyone was staring. He sat frozen until the man walked away. Someone else took the drum, and began dancing as the woman chanted.

Dietmar chuckled. "Way to be, Austen."

"I couldn't move, I couldn't think. Why did he do that?"

Laser smiled. "He honours you, Tom. The people know you are interested in how we live. They have seen you making notes. But don't worry—few *kabloonas* participate in our culture."

As others took a turn with the drum, Tom fidgeted. Was it too late to dance? Did he have the courage? Then, an outside door banged open, and cold air blew in. As it met the warmth in the community hall, the air turned into fog that billowed across the floor.

Tom glanced toward the open door, and his heart jumped. Standing there was Luke Yates, reeling back and forth. He was obviously drunk.

* * *

Yates stumbled onto the floor. "Stupid . . . Eskimos. I want . . . " He swayed, his red eyes searching the faces. "I want . . . *you*!"

Yates pointed at Junior, who sat near the stage. The singer had stopped her chant, and was looking at Yates with impassive eyes. The dancer laid down the drum and returned to his seat.

"*You* . . . " Yates weaved toward Junior. "Deny me . . . will you? I want a big white . . . Why don't you . . . ? I want . . . "

Pulling out a bottle of rum, Yates finished it off. After wiping his mouth, he threw the bottle against a wall. It shattered, and glass rained down.

The children had stopped their play. All eyes watched Yates.

"*Morons* . . . you're all morons . . . you're . . . "

Yates lurched toward the door.

"I hate . . . I hate . . . you . . . "

Then he was gone. For a moment, there was total silence, followed by the excited babbling of the southern teens. Tom looked at Junior, and then at the people in their colourful parkas. Sorrow was in their eyes.

Standing up, Tom walked on shaking legs toward the drum. Applause rang out from all sides. He saw faces suddenly grinning. The drum was decorated with the face of an Inuk; Tom picked it up, aware of his pulsating heart.

As the chant began from the stage, Tom danced. He felt awkward at first, pounding the drum, but soon his feet were moving faster and faster. When the song ended, he returned to his seat, grinning at the applause.

"Where's Junior?" he asked Mr. Cousins.

"He left." The teacher took a photo of the next dancer, and then said, "I feel sorry for that big guy, the way Yates insults his people. Junior must be steaming inside." He shook his head. "You've got to admire that Inuit self-control."

Tom stood up. "I think I'll head off, sir. Tomorrow I'm going on the land with the Mountie. We'll be out two nights."

"You're a lucky guy, Tom. I guess it's your Irish roots. Have fun, and stay out of trouble."

Outside the community hall, Tom looked for signs of Junior, but he was gone. Passing the hotel, he saw Luke Yates at the front desk, reading a message slip. Faith sat behind the desk, watching him.

Yates left the hotel. Keeping well behind, Tom followed him to the harbour. From the shelter of a house, he watched through his binoculars as Yates crossed the snow. He was walking toward the *Netsilik*.

Suddenly, Tom dashed from hiding and yelled, "Watch out!" Startled by the cry, Luke Yates turned to stare at him. "Run," Tom shouted. He pointed at the boat. "It's going to explode!"

* * *

Luke Yates stared at the *Netsilik*. Sparks were racing across the snow-bound deck of the boat. "It's a fuse," Tom yelled at Yates. "Run!"

The man took off fast. As he did, a massive explosion shook the night. The roof of the *Netsilik* blew straight up into the sky, and wood flew in every direction. Black smoke and orange flames billowed from the doomed vessel while the town echoed with the sound of the blast.

Knocked to the ground, Luke Yates lay motionless. Then he got slowly up, and staggered to Tom's side. He smelled of rum. "You saved my life, kid! I'd have been blown up."

"Why are you here?"

"I got a message about a hunting tag for sale. It said to meet at the boat. I figured the person didn't want to be seen."

"Was the message signed?"

Yates shook his head. "Anyway, kid, what's going on? Why are you here? Were you following me?"

"I was heading home," Tom replied. "It's lucky for you I saw the danger. Someone tried to kill you, and I'm not surprised. You've insulted everyone in town."

"So what?" Luke Yates spat on the ground. "They can't stop me, even with a bomb. I'll get a tag, and I'll kill a polar bear."

A large crowd quickly gathered to watch the remains of the *Netsilik* burn. After being questioned by the Mountie, Tom walked to the hotel. But he was unable to report in person to Sam, who was not feeling well. Faith was working the desk for him, so Tom ripped a page from his notebook and wrote a description of the night's events.

"Please give this to Sam," he said, sealing his report inside an Amundsen Hotel envelope. "ASAP."

"Huh?"

"As soon as possible."

"What is it?"

Tom shrugged. "Just something. But it's private."

Faith looked at the envelope, then at Tom. "Okay," she said. "Sam's sleeping now, but he'll get this in the morning. I promise."

The moment Tom left the hotel, the lights went off. The lobby was plunged into darkness. He squinted his eyes, trying to see Faith. But she had disappeared.

11

In the morning, Tom went with Dietmar and the twins to the Anglican church. It was a small wooden building with a bell tower. Snowmobiles were parked outside, and the minister stood by the door greeting his congregation.

Many people sat inside in their beautiful parkas. They smiled a welcome as Tom and his friends joined other teens from Winnipeg. Above the altar was a large tapestry displaying the syllabics of Inuktitut.

"Have you wondered about my name?" Moses whispered to Tom. "It was chosen from the Bible by my parents. It is a good name."

A choir enthusiastically led the singing of a hymn, prayers were said in Inuktitut, and the minister gave his sermon. Tom didn't understand the words, but was moved by the tears that rolled down the man's face.

"He's talking about the future," Rachel whispered. "He hopes the visit of such fine young people will bring us all closer together. Let us forget the time of fear, when the southerners controlled our lives. Instead, let us build our culture, and our faith."

Tara and Nicole, from Tom's class, concluded the service by singing an anthem, and everyone hugged goodbye at the door. The wind had picked up, whipping the fur that fringed Tom's parka hood.

"The world's coldest breezes," a woman grinned, climbing on to her snowmobile. As she buzzed away into the blinding white landscape, Tom put on his sunglasses. "One hour until the U-SAC debate," he exclaimed to his friends. "Let's watch it together, at the Mountie's."

Soon they were gathered in front of the TV, clutching mugs of tea. The room was packed and everyone cheered when Mrs. Austen was shown, seated at a table beside five other citizens. Across from them were the Prime Minister and his advisers.

"Mom looks nervous." Tom smiled. "It's her first brush with fame."

"Look at that red hair," said the Mountie's wife. "Just like her son."

"Mom's a member of Lawyers for Social Responsibility. Maybe that's why she was chosen for this panel."

"Is she against U-SAC?"

Tom laughed. "I'll say! It's all we hear about."

Prime Minister Dunbar was a natural for television. The colour of his eyes was enhanced by the blue shirt he wore with a stylish suit. He spoke with confidence about the merits of U-SAC in an opening statement, then handled the panel's questions with skill. The studio audience applauded him enthusiastically.

Following the debate, the TV commentator said, "James Dunbar has earned the trust of Canadians. People seem prepared to follow this Prime Minister anywhere, even into union with the United States. The PM's performance tonight was brilliant, and our early polling indicates U-SAC has now gained huge support."

Tom groaned. He believed the Prime Minister's scheme could be stopped, but only if the micro-cassette were found.

"I'm impressed with Judith Austen," said the commentator. "This fiery criminal lawyer from Winnipeg is well spoken, and a natural leader."

"Yes, Mom!"

"The debate's strongest moment came when she clashed with the PM on the subject of handguns. Let's watch it again."

The commentator looked at a screen. On it, Tom's mother was arguing with the Prime Minister. "The fact is," she said, "citizens of the United States have the constitutional right to bear arms, which means the right to defend themselves with guns. Will the people of U-SAC *all* have this right? Will Canadians be able to purchase handguns at a corner store?"

The Prime Minister's soothing reply was cut off by an angry Mrs. Austen. "Don't pretend the Americans will change their constitution to suit us! We're the little country, so they'll make the rules."

"True, but . . . "

"If your referendum wins, and Canada joins the States, will our citizens have the constitutional right to purchase handguns? Please answer my question!"

Prime Minister Dunbar whispered with an adviser. Then he said, "My own father died of a gunshot wound, Mrs. Austen. In your hometown, in fact." He looked directly at the audience. "I know the pain. I know the suffering. I will protect our citizens, in every way I can."

The audience burst into huge applause. Some rose to their feet, clapping and smiling.

Facing the camera, the commentator held up a copy of *People* magazine. Prime Minister Dunbar was on the cover, looking good. "With this kind of success," she said, "our PM is becoming a big name in Washington. Some day, he could be the first president of U-SAC."

* * *

Outside the house, the Mountie and Tom roped their gear onto a *komatik*. Whipped up by the wind, snow blew around them. "Your mother is wise," the Mountie said quietly. "Who controls the land, controls the future. If the referendum passes, Americans will decide all matters for us. My people have experience of losing control to *kabloonas*. We were powerless, so our needs were ignored."

Tom stopped his work to listen. "Weren't you angry about it? Didn't you want to punch someone?"

The Mountie shook his head. "Violence leads only to more violence. That is how wars begin, bringing terrible pain."

"But don't you ever get upset about things?"

"Of course." The Mountie smiled. "I feel anger, then I let it go. I know there is good and bad in each person. No one is perfect, so I forgive. In this way, my heart is peaceful."

The Mountie studied the wind-swept landscape. "This land of ours is a good one, Tom. In Canada, people live in harmony. We show the world the meaning of peace. If our country disappears, it will be lamented. Just like the lost civilization of Atlantis, Canada will never return."

"I won't let that happen!"

"Good for you. Our country needs kind and caring leaders. We must work together, the young and the old, to cherish our land, and protect it. Canada was a gift to us at birth, and we must pass this benefaction on safely to future generations."

* * *

Powering up his black SnowCat, the Mountie waved goodbye to the little kids at the window. Tom smiled at them. Seated behind the Mountie, he was warm inside a caribou parka and wolf-skin leggings.

As they bounced through town, various people called hello. Faith and Junior were outside the hotel speaking together with great intensity. Neither paid attention to the Mountie's snowmobile as it passed by. Watching over his shoulder, Tom saw Junior put his arms around Faith.

He glanced at the Mountie, wondering if he'd seen. But the man was concentrating on the horizon as they left town. Banging over drift after drift, the big machine roared across the white landscape. At last they stopped for a tea break, and Tom was able to stretch his legs.

"What's happening about that explosion?" he asked.

"An RCMP expert is arriving tomorrow from Yellowknife to assist in the investigation. Like you, I think it was a bomb. Unfortunately, this means our trip on the land will be shorter."

"There must be dozens of suspects. Everyone dislikes Yates."

"I met with him this morning," the Mountie said. "He refuses to leave Gjoa Haven. Mr. Yates tells me he's investigating a story."

"About what?"

"He did not say." The Mountie cut strips of raw caribou with his *ulu*. "Mr. Yates was drinking last night, which is against the law. Gjoa Haven is a dry town. I am considering action against him."

"What's a dry town?"

"No alcohol allowed. The people have voted for this. Many of the settlements are dry towns. We do not have the same problem with suicides as those settlements where alcohol is allowed."

Eating the meat, Tom began to sweat. "I feel hot," he said. "As if I've got a furnace burning inside."

"Your body is burning energy to keep warm." Standing up, the Mountie pointed. "Look, Tom. Caribou."

The animals were some distance away. Their heads were bent forward to the snow. "They're like reindeer," Tom said. "What are they eating?"

"Mosses and lichens hidden beneath the snow. The

covering is not deep—we actually get very little snow here."

"Do you have blizzards?"

The Mountie nodded. "High winds pick up the snow, and swirl it around. Such a ground blizzard can last for days. Many hunters have died. When someone is lost on the land, people in town barely sleep. Inuit and *kabloona*, we join together as a family, waiting for news. We share our prayers for the missing person, and we share the joy of a cherished friend's safe return. Or, we share our sorrow, if the worst has happened."

Tom thought of Franklin's men, staggering through this same wilderness until they died. He felt lonely. "I've heard that those British sailors became cannibals. Yuck, what a thought. I'd rather be eaten by a polar bear."

"Not me, thank you. Polar bears are ferocious. They run very fast, and we cannot escape up a tree."

As the Mountie packed their gear, Tom looked at the distant horizon. The weak afternoon sun shone above the frozen sea. "It's so silent out here."

The man smiled. "No car alarms. Your father would like that."

"You're right—they're his pet peeve." Tom took a photo of the desolate beauty. "The sun never shines in winter, eh? What's that like?"

"People kind of hibernate. They slow down, and sleep a lot. It is a good feeling to see the sun again."

"What about summer? I hear you get eternal sunshine."

"Everyone is busy. At three a.m. the sun is bright.

But we have no grass, only sand. It blows around, and bothers the eyes. I welcome the return of snow."

"Has your face ever been frozen?"

"Yes, and it was not pleasant. It felt like pliers, pinching my skin."

Travelling on, they reached the igloos at the ice-fishing site as the sky grew dark. Tom helped drag their gear into the biggest igloo, then watched the Mountie flick the short-wave radio's *on* switch.

"I like staying connected to the outside world," he explained. "Later tonight, we'll call Sam at the hotel. Just to say hello."

"Maybe tomorrow we can toss the harpoon, and do some ice fishing. Last time, the harpoon was kept in this igloo. I wonder where it's gone?"

The warmth of the Coleman stove made the igloo cosy as the Mountie cut caribou meat and dropped it into a boiling pot.

"I feel good," Tom said to the Mountie while writing in his notebook. "Earlier, I was kind of freaked. I got scared of the wilderness, or something. It was like a feeling of doom."

The Mountie nodded. "It gets lonely out here. But the spirits of my ancestors journey with us." He smiled gently at Tom. "You have eaten caribou with my family. Now you are a part of us."

Tom was very pleased. "Thank you," he said.

"Come outside. We will search for the Great Bear."

The black night was filled with stars. Moonlight glowed on the snow, which was silver, like a desert of the night. "Look directly above, Tom. There you see Ursa Major. The Greeks named this region *Arktikós*, meaning the land of the Great Bear." For long moments he was silent. "I am part of all that surrounds me—every living thing. In the jungles, in the deserts, in the cities, the people are my people. Others may live far away, but we share this world. I protect it, for them and for future generations. We must owe the young no apology."

He raised a hand. "Listen."

Tom strained his ears, but heard nothing. "What is it?"

"Someone is coming."

The Mountie was motionless, listening intently. Then Tom heard the sound, a distant buzzing. It grew louder as the bouncing headlight of a snowmobile appeared. "It's Luke Yates," Tom warned the Mountie. "Be careful."

The Ski-Doo roared to a stop. Throwing back his parka hood, Yates stared at the Mountie. "Well, cop? Where is it?"

"What do you mean, sir?"

"Don't mess with me, mister. Where's that hunting tag? I came miles into this emptiness to get it."

"Would you explain, please?"

"You sent a message, saying to meet here. Saying you'd found a tag for me. I fly home in two days, so stop wasting time. Give me the tag."

"I did not send a message, sir. I have nothing for you."

For a moment, Yates could only stare. His mouth moved, but no words came out. The night was electric with tension. Then, suddenly, he swore furiously, and brandished his fist.

"This is your fault!"

The Mountie said nothing.

"You lousy, no-good Eskimo. You make my life a misery. You and your smug rules! My hunting trip cost big money, and I haven't killed anything." Yates stormed away, then swung around and advanced again on the Mountie. His face was red with fury.

"I should get my gun, and shoot *you*." Foul words poured from his mouth. "I hate this place," Yates screamed, "and I hate *you*!"

The Mountie showed no emotion, but Tom's heart was beating fast. Anything could happen! Desperate for help, he remembered the ham radio and ran to the igloo.

Slithering inside, he grabbed the microphone. "Hello, hotel! Sam, help us! Get someone here—the Mountie's in danger, and . . ."

A hideous cry sounded from the night. Dropping the microphone, Tom crawled out of the igloo to a terrible sight. Under the glow of the moon, a man lay face down in the snow.

Quivering in his back was a harpoon.

12

Before Tom could react, the roar of a snowmobile split the silence. Scrambling to his feet, he ran toward the sound. Tom was in time to see the bouncing lights of a snowmobile escaping into the night. The rider was a dark shape, leaning over the controls.

The dead man's arms were spread wide in the snow. Kneeling over him was the Mountie. "What happened?" Tom cried. "Is that Yates—*dead*?"

The Mountie nodded. "Yates was walking to his snowmobile. A harpoon came from the darkness, and took him down." He stood up from examining the body. "The harpoon was thrown from behind our igloo. The killer must have hidden there, listening to every word we said."

Frost was whitening the dead man's hair. "I wonder what he'll find in the next life," Tom said.

"Perhaps forgiveness. His was a troubled soul."

The Mountie used Tom's camera to photograph the scene, then made extensive notes as they sipped tea and ate caribou. He tried to reach Gjoa Haven on the ham radio, but failed. "There must be a wire loose."

"I probably wrecked something, trying to reach Sam for help." Tom looked around at the darkness. "I had a look at the harpoon. It's the same one as our first trip here."

"Thank you for that information," the Mountie said, making a note. Using ropes, he secured the murder weapon and the victim to the *komatik*. "You take my SnowCat," he said to Tom. "I will follow on the dead man's Ski-Doo."

Although shaken by the death of Luke Yates, Tom liked being at the controls of the big machine with the RCMP crest on its side. His head whirled with thoughts and theories about Yates, and he was anxious to see Sam. Reaching town, he followed the Mountie to the RCMP office. Almost immediately, people came running. Rachel was among them.

"What happened?" she asked breathlessly. Moses began filming the scene with his video camera as a crowd quickly gathered. "Is that *Yates*?"

The Mountie approached. "I will take the dead man to the morgue at the nursing station. Tom, the hour is late. Try to sleep, and in the morning I will take your formal statement about the murder."

As he rode away on the snowmobile, Moses ran behind with his camera. "Your brother's getting some good stuff." Tom smiled at Rachel. "He's got a future in TV." He told her about the night's events.

"Any idea who escaped on the snowmobile?"

Tom shook his head. "It was yellow, but that's a popular colour for those machines. The person was just a dark shape. It could have been anyone." He sighed unhappily. "With Yates dead, I'll never find that micro-cassette."

"What do you mean?"

"Sorry, Rachel, I can't reveal too much. I've been looking in Gjoa for a micro-cassette hidden in a boat. But all the boats are swamped with snow, or blown up."

"Hey," Rachel exclaimed. "I know another boat!"

"You do?"

"Yes, in the museum."

"What kind—big, small?"

"Come on," Rachel cried. "I'll show you!"

* * *

Minutes later, they reached the town hall. It was in darkness. All around, snow glistened under the bright moon. Like other places in Gjoa, the door wasn't locked. Stepping inside, Rachel flicked on a pencil flashlight. The tiny beam of light moved slowly up a staircase to a wide hallway. It glittered against the glass of a large display cabinet. Above it hung a harpoon and a kayak; inside the case was caribou clothing and an ancient photograph of long-ago elders.

A map on the wall traced the routes of Franklin and other famous Arctic explorers. Nearby were volleyball trophies, and a display of T-shirts and baseball caps with the words *The Hamlet of Gjoa Haven*.

"You think the micro's in that kayak?" Tom whispered.

"No." Putting a finger to her lips, Rachel led Tom up the stairs. The flashlight beam led them to the display cabinet. Inside was a scale-model of an old-fashioned fishing boat with full sails.

"That is the boat I mean," Rachel whispered. "It is a scale model of Amundsen's boat, the *Gjoa*."

Rachel stopped speaking, and her light snapped out. "What was that sound?"

"I didn't hear anything."

"Sssh." Rachel was motionless. "Tom, there is someone in this building. I hear movement."

Tom pushed back his parka hood. Now he could hear it, a faint scuffling sound. Crouching beside Rachel, he tried to see through the darkness.

A door handle squealed.

Then he heard feet, moving stealthily through the darkness.

"Got you," Rachel yelled, flicking on the flashlight. "Don't move!" The beam jumped through the darkness to show Faith, her mouth open in an *ooooh* of surprise.

"Faith," Rachel cried. "What are you doing here?"

"I was walking home and saw a flashlight inside. I wanted to make sure my cleaning materials weren't being tampered with, so I slipped in the back door. I wasn't taking any chances." She stared at them. "Now tell me—what are *you* doing here?"

Quickly, Tom explained about the death of Yates. When he was finished, Faith frowned. "But why are you here?" she demanded.

"I'm looking for a micro-cassette, and it may be hidden in the model of the Gjoa. That's all I can say."

Faith studied his face. "Okay," she said at last, "let's test your theory." Using her key, Faith opened the display cabinet and lifted out the green and yellow model. "The deck is hinged. Open it, Tom."

The sails tilted as Tom looked under the deck. "There *is* something in here," he whispered in excitement. "And guess what? It's a micro-cassette!"

* * *

At that moment, the outside door opened. Shocked by the sudden noise, Tom almost yelled in horror. Rachel swung the flashlight beam to the door, and for a moment they clearly saw Junior. Then he was gone, slamming the door behind him.

Tom and Rachel ran to open the door. "Look," Tom exclaimed. "Junior's escaping from town! He's got his dog team."

"What do you mean, escaping?"

"I think," Tom whispered, "that he's the one who killed Luke Yates."

"How horrible." Rachel looked at the night. "Junior could live on the land a long time. Unlike a snow-mobile, his dog team won't run short of fuel. Junior may never return."

Faith was waiting for them beside the display case. The *Gjoa* was back in its place, and the glass door was closed. "I don't know why Junior ran away," Faith said. "That's very strange behavior. We work together cleaning this place."

"Where's the micro?" Tom asked.

Faith fished it from her jeans pocket. "There's no identifying information—it's probably just a blank tape. Anyway, I don't know why it's so important."

Pocketing the micro-cassette, Tom turned to Rachel. "Let's go, okay? Thanks for your help, Faith."

"No problem."

Tom and Rachel walked together through the snow-packed streets. The night was black, with some light from the windows of homes and the occasional passing snowmobile. Saying goodbye to Rachel, Tom went into the hotel. There was a lot to tell Sam.

The building was closed for the night, but the door was unlocked. At the front desk, Tom rang a bell. A few minutes later, Sam came from his living quarters. Looking sad, he glanced at the photograph of Faith.

Tom smiled. "She must be proud of you, eh?"

"I'm forbidden to tell Faith I'm CSIS, Tom. If she knew, the agency's secret northern operations would be vulnerable. My life could even be at risk."

"Could she have learned somehow, maybe from Junior? He's your best friend—does he know you're CSIS?"

Sam shook his head. "Anyway, Tom, I'm glad you're here. I appreciated your report about last night's explosion. I heard that Luke Yates has been murdered. What can you tell me?"

Tom gave Sam a full report on the night's horrifying events. He finished by saying, "Almost anyone could have killed Luke Yates, but unfortunately I think it was Junior—which is really sad."

"Why Junior?"

"Yates was incredibly cruel to Junior and his people. I mean, there's a limit to self-restraint. Junior finally blew his top, and killed Yates. Then he escaped from town—I saw him. He probably wanted that harpoon from the museum, to use for hunting."

Sam sighed. "I hope it's not true, Tom. He's my friend."

Tom remembered Junior putting his arms around Faith, but he didn't say anything.

"But," Sam said, "I'll get CSIS to run a check on Junior. While that's happening, I'll contact your Dad on the secure line. Get some sleep, and let's meet here in the morning."

"Is there anything more from CSIS on Yates?"

Sam nodded. "There's a top RCMP officer arriving on the morning flight. Luke Yates was about to be arrested."

"I wish I'd seen that happen." Unable to contain his excitement any longer, Tom proudly displayed his trophy. "Look, Sam! I've found the missing micro-cassette."

Sam was astonished. His mouth dropped open, and his eyes stared at Tom. "You are *brilliant*!"

Tom beamed.

"But wait a minute." Sam studied the micro. "Nothing's written on it. This could be any cassette."

Tom's eyes were bright with excitement. "It was hidden in a boat in Gjoa. It's *got* to be the missing micro!"

"Let's find out."

Sam quickly removed a tape from the hotel's answering machine, snapped in the tiny cassette and pushed *Play*. They heard nothing, and Tom's heart fell. It was blank.

Then a familiar baritone was heard from the machine. *What is it, Decker?* said the voice. *I'm entertaining important people.*

"Yes!" Tom punched the air. "That's the Prime Minister for sure. We've nailed James Dunbar!"

Grinning, Sam shook Tom's hand. "I'm signing you for CSIS," he joked. "You're an ace sleuth."

Together, they listened to the entire conversation. "The PM is finished," said Sam. "So is U-SAC, I'd say. He's betrayed the people."

"What'll we do now?"

"I'll contact CSIS headquarters immediately. Meet me here at 0700 hours, and I'll tell you what they've decided. In the meantime, not one word to anyone."

"You bet." Tom cracked the air with a huge yawn. "I've got some sleeping to do. Suddenly, I'm exhausted."

* * *

Inside his host's house, Tom peeled off layers of clothing. The Mountie's parka wasn't on its peg, so he was probably still at his office. Tea-Granny was watching the late-night news; the sound was off. Her wrinkled face broke into a warm smile. *"Teagukpin?"*

"Thanks, but no."

A picture of the Prime Minister appeared on the TV screen. "May I?" Tom asked, turning up the volume.

"With only days remaining until the referendum," the news announcer said, "union with the United States seems certain. A poll released today names James Dunbar the most trusted prime minister in the history of Canada. The same poll indicates that the referendum will pass easily. The Prime Minister is greatly admired, and has successfully silenced the critics of U-SAC."

"He won't be admired for much longer," Tom said with great satisfaction.

After the news, Tea-Granny climbed the stairs to bed, but Tom remained on the couch. Flipping through the family scrapbook, he studied the pages about Junior's army career.

Frowning, Tom closed his eyes to think. There was an important connection in the scrapbook, but he couldn't quite get it. He was *so* tired. He began to snore.

In his dreams, Tom drifted through a frozen landscape. Darkness and snow were everywhere. An ancient sailing ship was trapped forever by ice. Skeletons rose up from the frozen land, their skulls thick with frost. A bony finger beckoned Tom to join them. "It's too cold," he moaned. "Leave me alone."

Tom woke from the dream, shivering. He looked around—where was he? Shaking his head, he tried to concentrate. Had the Mountie come home?

At that moment, outside the house, the silent night was shattered by a terrible blast. Tom sat up on the couch, eyes wide. "What was that?" he cried.

Running to the door, he threw it open. At the top of the hill, fire raged. The storage tank had blown apart, filling the night with roaring flames.

13

Fire consumed the night. The walls of houses reflected the flames that leapt into the sky. Tom grabbed a jacket and ran outside. People were everywhere, yelling and pointing at the flames. Tom could see the Mountie near the fire, organizing help.

A Polaris snowmobile roared out from behind the twins' house. The rider called to Tom, and gestured urgently. It was Sam. He stopped the Polaris. "Listen carefully, Tom. Your life is in danger—we must act fast."

"What do you mean?"

"Junior is ZULU-1."

Tom was shocked. He couldn't speak.

"Get your parka, fast. Your Dad wants you in hiding. Junior has killed once, and he could kill again. He may figure you've got the micro-cassette."

•

"But where is it now?"

"With me." Sam showed Tom the micro, then returned it to his pocket. "At dawn, a planeload of reinforcements is arriving from Yellowknife. You and I can take refuge at the ice-fishing igloos, then return to Gjoa in the morning."

The thunder of the fire filled the night. Black smoke billowed toward the stars. "But why the explosion?" Tom asked.

"To create a diversion. With everyone focused on the fire, it's a lot easier to kill you."

"I'll get my parka."

Dashing inside, Tom grabbed some paper and scribbled FOR INTEREST SAY HI. IN GLOVES LIVE OILY OINKY SLOTHS. After wiggling into the big caribou parka, he pulled on his *kamiks* and ran to join Sam.

Out on the frozen sea, they stopped to look at Gjoa Haven. The houses of the tiny hamlet seemed defenceless, huddled together under the roaring flames. Sam shook his head. "What a disaster for these good people."

"I can't believe Junior would be so cruel."

"I made a big mistake," Sam admitted. "I should have realized my buddy could be ZULU-1. Like you, I wanted to believe the hitman was Luke Yates."

"Why did Junior kill him? Because of his racism?"

"Probably not. Yates was sniffing around Gjoa, looking for signs of a hitman. I think Junior got nervous, and killed to protect his secret." Sam cranked up the engine. "We'd better keep going."

As they travelled on, the wind roared past Tom's face. The night sky was beautiful, but he could only think about Junior. The killer could be anywhere, and probably he was armed.

"Junior may have that gun and the silencer," Tom called to Sam.

"No," the man yelled back. "Luke Yates found it, at the dump. He moved it to another hiding place."

"That's what I saw Yates find? The gun?"

"Yes. It belonged to ZULU-1."

"How do you know?"

"We're almost there," Sam called. "Then I'll tell you."

The ice-fishing igloos appeared ahead. They looked lost and unhappy, alone under the vast sky. When they stopped, Sam raised his face to the wind. "The weather is changing."

"For the better?"

"For the worse. Let's get settled in."

Before long, they had made themselves cosy in the largest igloo. There was warmth from a hissing Coleman stove, and good tea to drink. "I hope there isn't another harpoon around here," Tom said. "I keep hearing Yates scream, when he went down."

Sam didn't reply. He was concentrating on the ham radio, trying to get it fixed. "Remember at the James Bay Inn?" he asked. "When you were carrying that coffee pot? Did you see my reflection, when I left Room 306?"

Cold fear gripped Tom's throat. "What do you mean?"

Sam grinned. "When you listened at the door of Room 306, Tom, I was in there. I was the hitman." He chuckled, pleased with himself. "I'm ZULU-1."

* * *

Sam casually poured himself another mug of tea. "Want some?" he asked. "You're allowed a last meal before dying—any requests? Caribou stew?"

"I . . . You can't . . . "

"You shouldn't have snooped around, Tom. Your death will be a tragedy. I saw your Mom on TV—she's gorgeous. She'll be crying those beautiful eyes out."

"You'd never kill me."

"This is about money, Tom. You must die, to protect my secret."

Cold sweat soaked Tom's body. "You killed for that stupid micro-cassette. *Why?*"

"Blackmail. The Prime Minister doesn't want this tape released to the media. He'll pay me to keep it a secret." Sam chuckled. "We're talking big, big bucks."

"You kill for money? That's so disgusting."

Sam's face went red. "Watch your mouth."

"Why's the money so important? To buy that Rolex you wear? You'd kill someone for a watch?"

Sam laughed. "Don't be stupid, Tom. The cash is for cocaine." He wiped at his eyes. "Coke is so great. It makes me super powerful. Just give me a little snort of my friend and I rule the world. I'm number one—I can do anything."

"Is . . . " Tom could barely speak the words. "Does . . . Faith . . . ?"

"No." Sam shook his head. "Faith is the kindest person I ever met. Her people have become my family. She's a true innocent." He grinned. "Faith says cocaine is like a monkey on my back, and it won't let go. But she doesn't understand what coke gives me. With it, I can do anything. I'll get big money by blackmailing the Prime Minister, and then I'll have my power forever." He gestured at his pack. "I've got some with me. Want to try coke before you die? You might as well."

Tom ignored the suggestion. "Is that how you wrecked your eyes and nose? Snorting cocaine?"

Sam said nothing.

"I bet you framed Junior. Your friend!"

Sam shrugged. "I needed to protect myself. I created several false identities, including Samuel G. White, CSIS agent." Smiling, he poured more tea. "That's good," he said, smacking his lips. "As part of my protection I picked a fall guy, just in case. Junior was perfect."

Sam took another gulp. "Several years ago, Junior was framed for a murder. He spent a long time in prison, then was released when the true criminal confessed." Sam shook his head. "The poor guy, the experience left permanent scars. Junior is terrified of prison bars."

The killer casually studied his fingernails. "I told Junior he was suspected of murdering Luke Yates, and he panicked. As I'd expected, he decided to escape from town. I promised to meet him at the Franklin Cairn with supplies. Instead, I'll shoot Junior with my rifle and get rid of his body. The chief suspect in the Luke Yates harpooning will never return from the wilderness. That file will remain inactive, and life will go on."

"What about *my* death? It will be investigated."

"You're a kid from the south. You wandered away

from the igloo and froze to death. It happens, what can I say? The Mountie may smell a rat, but so what?"

"It's stupid to kill me! I've never hurt you."

"You've got to die, Tom. You're the only person alive who knows the truth about this micro. I lied about talking to your father. He doesn't know a thing." Sam grinned. "Too bad, eh? You actually found ZULU-1 and the micro. You're a hero, but your family will never know."

"Why'd you pick the code name ZULU-1?"

"I didn't—it was Decker's choice. You'd better ask him, when you get to Heaven."

Outside the igloo, Tom saw snow blowing past the Polaris. The machine could easily carry him to safety, but how could he get to it? "Can I use the biffy? I'll come right back."

Sam chuckled. "Not a chance."

"I need to know something," Tom said, hoping to somehow reach the Polaris. "Was it you at the storage tank?"

The killer nodded. "When you arrived from Winnipeg, I got worried. You're a bright kid, but too snoopy. At the tank, I was confirming how I'd attach explosives, in case I needed to create a diversion. Which is exactly what happened tonight."

"I nearly fell to my death. You didn't even try to help me!"

Sam shrugged. "It was your choice to be there, Tom. I wasn't about to blow my cover by rescuing you."

"I remember that you and Junior were in the same army demolitions unit. That's where you learned about explosives."

Sam sighed. "This week's been a nightmare. You were after a hitman, and so was Yates. I tell you, I lost some sleep."

"Good!"

Sam ignored Tom's comment. "I shut you down by claiming to be CSIS. That was easy, but Yates remained a problem. I saw him snooping around the hotel, then checking other places in town. I knew he was looking for a hidden gun."

"Why wasn't it with the micro-cassette?"

"That model boat is too small to hide a gun."

"You used Faith's key to open the cabinet?"

Sam nodded. "Anyway, Yates eventually located my weapon at the dump. Smart reasoning, but that moment sealed his fate."

The man's watery eyes stared at Tom. "I lured Yates to the boat, expecting to blow him apart. But he escaped death," Sam said resentfully, "because of you."

Tom glanced longingly at the night, just outside. Escape was so near, yet so far. Then he was startled to see a movement. Desperate for time, Tom searched for another question. "You arrived at the igloos first, and disabled the radio?"

Sam nodded. "Then I waited in hiding. Yates had the pistol and the silencer, so I decided to use the harpoon. I've got a throwing arm—I won all those javelin golds. Knowing the Mountie planned to overnight at the igloos with you, I lured Yates here in search of a hunting tag."

"People will know you killcd mc."

"I'm a smart guy, Tom." Sam finished his tea. "I figure all the angles. I'll have a sad story to tell, when I return home with your body roped to my *komatik*. How you panicked after the explosion, and figured Junior wanted to kill you. How I reluctantly agreed to help you hide on the land. How you wandered away from the igloo, and perished tragically."

He smiled. "I'm leaving now with the Coleman stove. I'll ride to the Franklin Cairn and shoot Junior, then return here. Your body will resemble a large ice cube."

"The Mountie will get you!"

"He needs proof, Tom. But there isn't any."

A girl's voice was suddenly heard. "Want to bet on that?"

Tom and Sam both looked toward the sound. Someone knelt outside the entrance to the igloo holding a video camera. It was Rachel—and she was taping them.

"It's all on video," she told Sam. "Your whole scheme."

* * *

With a snarl, Sam scrambled out of the igloo. Quickly, Tom pulled on his parka and followed. The wind was harsh, the night black. Snow swirled around the igloos. Rachel dodged among them, trying to escape from Sam.

Racing across the snow, Tom threw himself at Sam's legs. They both went down hard. Rachel pulled Tom to his feet. "Hurry! We must get away."

Running from the igloos, they passed Moses. He was crouched on the snow, taping with his Sony.

"My brother backed me up with his own camera," Rachel cried.

Dietmar waited at the controls of the twins' snowmobile. Tom glanced back at Sam—he was getting painfully to his feet. "He can't catch us."

"Not on foot," Rachel said, "but his Polaris is powerful. Let's keep moving."

Rachel climbed on behind Dietmar, and Tom knelt on the *komatik* with Moses. The boy continued to shoot the scene as they escaped across the snow, feeling every bump.

"I saw you outside the igloo," Tom shouted to Rachel. "I tried to keep Sam talking."

"After the explosion," she called back, "I looked for you, but found only your code." She laughed. "Oily oinky sloths? Where'd you get *that*?"

Tom grinned. "I had to think fast."

"I talked to my brother and Dietmar, and we decided to follow. When we approached the igloos, I saw Sam's Polaris. I sneaked up on the igloo, just in case of trouble."

"Thank goodness for that," Tom replied. "But there's still a problem. Sam's got the micro-cassette." He looked at the distant igloos. "He's not chasing us. Let's see what happens."

Dietmar stopped the machine. The wind drove hard pellets of snow across the ridged landscape, stinging Tom's face like broken glass. Moses raised powerful binoculars to his eyes. "He's going northwest on the Polaris."

"Maybe he's heading for the Franklin Cairn," Tom said. "He wants to kill Junior."

"We've got to help Junior," Moses exclaimed. "Let's follow Sam at a distance. Keep the headlight out, Dietmar."

Staying well back, they followed the bouncing light on Sam's snowmobile across the frozen sea. Then, without warning, they were surrounded by snow. Lifted by the wind, it rose into their faces and swirled against their bodies. It was everywhere, swarming like white bees, sticking to the fur of Tom's parka, clogging his vision.

"Stop the machine," Moses yelled. "This is a ground blizzard! We must make an igloo, fast."

Fumbling under the snow-coated caribou skins on the *komatik*, Moses pulled out some large *panas*. He passed a knife to Rachel, and they began hacking out snow blocks. Their backs were to the wind, their parkas white with the coarse grains.

Working together, Tom and Dietmar lifted the blocks into place. Tom was shaking with the cold; he had to force his muscles to keep working. He felt bare to the wind, his parka defeated by its power. The snow hissed past, forming drifts that immediately blew into new shapes. The wind was a steady roar, high above.

With the last block in place, Rachel and Moses sliced out an entrance. Inside the igloo Tom and Dietmar helped block the entrance with snow, then spread out caribou robes from the *komatik*. Rachel lit candles, and the air began to warm.

"Good work, everyone," Moses said.

Tom wriggled his toes and banged his hands together, restoring the circulation. "Sam's out there somewhere. He's got a rifle."

"Sam will need more than a gun in this blizzard," Moses replied. "He needs a really good prayer."

"I'm hungry," Dietmar said. "There's a Coleman on the *komatik*. I'll get it, and some food." Punching a hole in the snow that blocked the entrance, he crawled out of the igloo and was lost in the blizzard.

"I hope he'll be okay," Rachel said.

Moses smiled fondly at his sister. "Dietmar will be fine."

The white shape of Dietmar wriggled into the igloo. He blocked the entrance with snow, then got the stove working. Before long they were ferociously devouring caribou strips and huge portions of Mr. Noodles. "I've never been so hungry," Tom said. "Is there more?"

Dietmar nodded. "Sure, I'll just . . . "

At that moment, a fist smashed through the snow blocking the entrance. As everyone yelled in shock, a man struggled into the igloo.

"It's Junior," Tom yelled. "Look out—he's got a harpoon!"

14

The friends cowered back, terrified by the sight of the weapon. Junior stared at them. "You guys? I thought I'd found Sam."

"Don't kill us," Dietmar cried.

"No chance of that," Junior laughed.

"But why are you here?" Tom asked.

"Just what I was about to ask you." He smiled. "Listen, I am so hungry."

"How about some Mr. Noodles?"

"Sounds good. But first I'll settle my dog team." After some time, Junior returned inside and blocked up the entrance with snow. Brushing back his parka hood, he made himself comfortable on a caribou skin. Outside, the huskies howled unhappily. "Sam said to meet at the Franklin Cairn, but he didn't show up. I was so nervous, back in Gjoa, that I was only half listening. I thought maybe I'd got the meeting place wrong, and we were supposed to meet at the ice-fishing site. I was travelling there when the blizzard struck. I tried to keep going, thinking I could reach the igloos. Then I found this one, and figured Sam was inside."

"Is that why you've got that harpoon?" Tom asked. "For self-protection?"

Junior nodded. "I've always wondered about Sam's mysterious trips south, and his expensive collection of laser discs. Hotel clerks don't make big money. I wasn't sure I trusted Sam, even though Faith did. But love is blind, right?"

"Not necessarily," Dietmar said, glancing at Rachel. She smiled shyly.

"Faith knew about Sam's addiction to coke," Junior said. "She turned to me for advice. I tried to help, but Sam was really hooked. Getting started was easy for him, but stopping was impossible."

"Sam was planning to kill you," Tom said. He told Junior about his own narrow escape from the killer. "Rachel and Moses have the proof of Sam's guilt on their video cameras."

Junior finished his Mr. Noodles, drank some tea, and then said, "I'm going to check my dogs. I won't be long."

After he'd left the igloo, Tom said, "I wonder what's happened to Sam? Could he build an igloo, by himself?"

"Possibly," Moses replied. "But he'd have trouble, working alone in this blizzard." He chewed thoughtfully on a caribou strip. "Sam will try to reach Gjoa on the Polaris."

"Unless he's doubled back," Rachel said. "He could have returned to the ice-fishing igloos for shelter."

"If Junior found this igloo," Tom said, "Sam could, too."

Dietmar's face turned pale. "Surely you're joking, Austen."

"Franklin's men died here. Anything's possible in this wilderness."

Moses smiled. "It's not wilderness to Rachel and me. It's our home."

Junior crawled into the igloo. "The dogs don't like this blizzard. But they're burrowed down. They'll be okay."

"I saw you at the museum," Tom said. "Were you after the harpoon?"

Junior nodded. "When I saw you, I got scared and took off fast. I already had one harpoon, but I wanted another. I figured I'd be hunting on the land a long time."

"Was it horrible in prison? It looks bad in movies."

For a moment, Junior closed his eyes. "It was the worst possible experience. But my spirit wouldn't die. I knew I was innocent, and I was determined to survive."

The teens listened quietly.

"When the real criminal confessed, I was released to freedom." Junior's voice shook with emotion. "I returned to Nunavut, to my people, but I have never forgotten that prison."

For many hours, the blizzard howled past outside. Tom slept poorly, his nightmares filled with weapons of death. Whenever he opened his eyes, the harpoon was close by in Junior's hand.

Eventually, the constant roaring stopped. The wind was gone. After a meal, they kicked their way outside. Drifts of snow were everywhere; the sky was gray. Nothing could be seen.

"Where's our Ski-Doo?" Dietmar said.

"Buried," Junior replied.

"What about the poor huskies?" Tom said. "I don't see them!"

Junior dug into the snow. "The dogs are used to this weather. They can breathe fine, even buried under snow." The black eyes and big muzzle of a husky appeared. Standing up from his little cave, the dog pressed its face against Junior, greeting him. Its tail wagged happily.

Junior dug out the remaining dogs. Standing up, they shook the snow from their bodies and yapped eagerly for food. Meanwhile, the teens had begun digging out the Ski-Doo and its *komatik*. They were still sweating from the task when everything was ready for the journey home.

A buzzing was heard in the misty distance. It grew louder, and Tom wondered if Sam was approaching on the Polaris. But it was the Mountie, who waved as he pulled up on his SnowCat.

"I've found you! We've been so worried." He stepped off the machine. "Several search parties are out."

Tom and the others described the night's events. When they'd finished, the Mountie smiled at his son. "Last night, Sam told me you'd confessed to killing Luke Yates. I didn't believe it was true."

"Thank you," Junior said quietly. He turned to the others. "Who's travelling with me to Gjoa? Tom Austen?"

"For sure!"

After Tom found a space on the *komatik*, Junior cracked a huge whip above the dogs. They took off running, yapping with excitement. Each was on a separate trace, spread out like a fan. "They love running," Junior called back to Tom. "*Hey—ho*," he cried to the dogs. "*Hey—ho!*"

Holding tight, feeling each drift they crossed, Tom looked at Dietmar and Moses on the nearby *komatik* being towed by Rachel on the Ski-Doo. Above their heads, a snowy owl glided past, then beat its short wings and was gone. The land was white and the sky was gray; Tom was amazed that Junior could travel with such confidence in a landscape without any signposts to guide the way.

Junior pointed toward a distant, ivory-coloured shape. Puzzled, Tom squinted his eyes. The figure was moving across the landscape, running on powerful legs. "It's a polar bear," he cried. "I can't believe my eyes!"

As though hearing Tom's voice, the polar bear paused. Its big head turned in their direction. Through his binoculars, Tom saw ferocious teeth in the bear's blue-black mouth. It snuffled the wind, then bounded away.

"I'm glad you've seen *nanook*," Junior said. "Those bears move fast, up to 25 miles per hour when they're chasing prey."

Tom was amazed at his good fortune in seeing the polar bear. If only he hadn't lost control of the micro-cassette, life would have been perfect.

Again, Junior pointed at a distant shape. Wishing he'd brought his camera, Tom waited for a beautiful bear to bound gracefully across the frozen barrens. But as they approached the shape, it remained motionless—a white shadow on the white land.

"What is it?" Rachel called, as Junior stopped his dog team. Everyone stood up, knocking snow from their caribou parkas. They stared at the drift-covered mound, wondering what it could be.

Junior brushed away snow, and they saw black metal. Then the name *Polaris* became visible. Next they saw Sam's face. He lay beside his snowmobile, frozen to death.

* * *

"He tried to outrun the blizzard," Junior commented.

Searching in Sam's pockets, the Mountie found the micro-cassette. "The cocaine made him take foolish chances."

"Did you know he was using that stuff?" Tom asked.

"No," the Mountie replied. "I guess Sam was clever at hiding his secret."

"I knew about it," Junior said, "because Faith asked for my help in getting Sam off cocaine. I talked to him about my experiences with coke, but it didn't help."

Dietmar looked at Junior. "You've done cocaine?"

"When I went down south a few years ago, people told me cocaine would make me feel like a god, in total control of everything and everyone, so I did some. It's true, you do think you're the coolest person alive—until you come down again. Then you just feel rotten."

Tom glanced at the Mountie. He was listening attentively to his son.

"When I did coke," Junior said, "I felt like a big success story, but the feeling lasted only a short time. The exhilaration was followed by this dead, flat emptiness. That's why it's addictive—you ache to feel the power again."

Junior looked at Sam's dead face. "Finally, I realized that cocaine is for losers. There's no good way forward, it's just a downward spiral. I don't judge others for what they do, but I made a personal choice to give up coke. I told this to Sam, but he wouldn't listen. When he died, he was probably high on cocaine, in the middle of a nightmare, but still thinking he was a god."

* * *

Journeying home on the *komatik*, Tom did his best to ignore Sam's frozen body at his side. Smoke was rising into the pale sky as they approached Gjoa Haven; the ruins of the storage tank still smouldered.

A giant plane descended loudly into the airport. "What's with the army transport?" Tom asked.

"The Armed Forces got the fire under control," the Mountie explained. "Those tankers are bringing in fuel. The government is providing emergency supplies until the storage tank can be rebuilt."

"Was anyone hurt in the explosion?"

"Happily, no."

"Then things are turning out okay," Tom said, "and

there's more excitement to come. Just wait until that micro-cassette is public knowledge."

* * *

Late the next day, Tom and Tea-Granny were watching television together. As usual, the house was crowded with visiting relatives. On the screen, a news announcer suddenly appeared.

"I have a bulletin," she said. Looking excited, she quickly put a radio receiver into her ear. Somewhere off camera, a voice yelled, *This is political dynamite!*

Ignoring this interruption, the announcer breathlessly said, "There's been a major breakthrough in the investigations into the murders of Blake Decker and Professor Dunbar. We believe the Prime Minister may be involved."

She listened to the radio receiver.

"We're going live to Winnipeg, where the police have begun a press conference."

Tom's father was seen, surrounded by reporters. Dozens of microphones were in his face. "A warrant has been issued for the arrest of Prime Minister James Dunbar," said Inspector Austen. "He will be charged in connection with his father's death."

The reporters all shouted questions. The loudest was, "Can you prove it?"

Inspector Austen held up a micro-cassette. "Thanks to some courageous people up north, proof now exists. The Prime Minister must answer for his actions."

The announcer appeared on camera. "We take you live to Ottawa. Carys Evans is standing by."

The network's chief political correspondent appeared. Behind her were the Parliament Buildings, spotlit as evening came to the nation's capital. The Peace Tower was framed by sunset colours.

"This is an amazing story," Carys Evans said. "I've just learned the Prime Minister has resigned. He'll be leaving the Parliament Buildings any minute now."

Television lights glared on a waiting police car. It was surrounded by hordes of reporters, all shouting questions as James Dunbar was rushed to the vehicle.

"He looks scared," Tom said.

As the car struggled away from the reporters, Carys Evans said, "I've never seen anything like this! Prime Minister Dunbar has fallen, the victim of arrogance, the victim of overweening pride."

The Mountie shook hands with Tom. "You have accomplished a great deal, Tom. Perhaps you have even changed history."

* * *

The next day, Tom was packing for the trip to Winnipeg. He was feeling sad; he would really miss his new friends.

Downstairs, Tea-Granny waited with a gift for Tom. It was a ring, carved from ivory, showing a snowy owl with its wings spread wide. "Thank you," Tom said, hugging her frail body. Tears were streaming down her face, and he was also crying. "Thank you!"

Outside, Tom and the Mountie roped his gear to the *komatik*. "You must return, Tom," the man said quietly. "You have become part of us."

Tom nodded, a lump in his throat. "I'll be back."

As they roared through town, he looked at the houses and thought about the good times he had enjoyed in Gjoa Haven. "I know what keeps this place warm," he called to the Mountie. "The people."

Lots of snowmobiles were parked outside the airport terminal. The tiny departure lounge was jammed. Rachel was crying as she hugged Dietmar goodbye. There were tears on many faces.

"Guess what, Austen?" Dietmar grinned. "Mom phoned last night. If I want to return here when I've finished school, she'll pay for the plane fare. She's glad I'm so happy."

"That's wonderful news."

Moses put his arm around Dietmar. "This is my brother. He is an Inuk now."

Dietmar beamed with pride.

Tom saw Faith enter the building, and went to say goodbye. "I'm sorry you lost your boyfriend," he said.

"Thank you," Faith replied, smiling sadly. "But I lost Sam long ago. The cocaine drained away his life, and then it killed him."

The Mountie beckoned to Tom, and they went outside together. The air was crisp and clear. Sunshine sparkled on the snow. The Mountie looked at the scene for a moment, then spoke.

"In our language, Tom, there is no word for goodbye. We are always a part of those we know and love. Your spirit has joined with all of ours." He shook Tom's hand. "Until we meet again."

"Thank you," Tom said, gripping the Mountie's hand. "I'm very proud to know you."

* * *

A week later, Tom was back at the Winnipeg Convention Centre. Instead of slaving over dirty pots, he was on stage. With him were Dietmar and the twins, who'd come south for the occasion. The friends were smiling and waving as a huge crowd cheered and whistled.

U-SAC was dead, and Canada would not be joining the United States. The referendum had been defeated by voters outraged at James Dunbar's betrayal of their trust. The capacity crowd at the convention centre had just seen the referendum result announced on the giant television screens, and they were applauding the young heroes, whose recovery of the micro-cassette had led to the end of the corrupt Prime Minister and his sinister plans.

As news cameras lit their faces, Dietmar grinned at Tom. "So this is fame. I could get used to it."

* * *

When the fantastic evening ended, Tom drove home with his family. Everyone was in a good mood—especially his Dad. Liz was humming a tune as their car approached River Heights. "I can't wait to phone Zoltan, and tell him about tonight."

"Will you go dancing on the weekend?" Tom asked.

"I doubt it! Zoltan can't dance."

"I know," Tom said. "He told me about his two left feet, but I'd forgotten when Sam said you'd been out dancing together. I should have realized he was lying about phoning my family."

"How'd he know Zoltan's name?"

"He heard me mention it at the Amundsen Hotel."

Liz turned to her mother. "Were the rumours true about CanSell?"

Passing lights shone on Mrs. Austen's face. "Yes," she replied. "James Dunbar was secretly involved with the scheme. Now that U-SAC is defeated, CanSell hasn't a chance. Our rivers are safe."

Mr. Austen glanced at her. "The world needs political leaders like you, sweetheart. People who want to help others. You're so compassionate, you'd make a wonderful Prime Minister."

Liz and Tom beamed at her. "That's a great idea," Tom said. "Go for it, Mom."

When Mrs. Austen didn't reply, Liz smiled. "We'll convince you, Mom. Just wait and see."

* * *

Arriving home, Tom climbed the stairs to his attic office. On the door, a faded sign warned KEEP OUT! THIS MEANS YOU. A slip of paper remained wedged in the door frame, so there'd been no intruders.

The ceiling seemed lower these days. Tom studied the faces of Canada's Most Wanted Criminals, then sat at his trusty computer. Opening a file, he began a letter to his cousin Duncan in Newfoundland.

I can't wait to tell you, he wrote, *about what happened in the Arctic. I think this story should be called THE INUK MOUNTIE ADVENTURE, in honour of the people I met up there. Anyway, it all began when I got this terrible job at the convention centre . . .*

About the Author

RON COUSINS

Eric Wilson on King William Island

To research this book, Eric Wilson accompanied a group of teenagers on a visit to Gjoa Haven on King William Island. Eric then spent several months carefully planning his story before he began writing the first draft. This was read by volunteer student editors, who provided Eric with valuable suggestions that helped him enormously as he rewrote his mystery.

The adventures of Tom and Liz Austen are followed by fans of all ages across Canada and abroad in countries like Spain and Japan. Voted 1992 Author of the Year by the Canadian Booksellers Association "for introducing children to the different regions of Canada," Eric Wilson has shown many young people the delights of reading.

HEY, KIDS!

Thanks to you, Eric Wilson has sold a million copies of his books. To celebrate, we have created

The Eric Wilson Million-Copy Man Contest

Four fabulous prizes!

The Grand Prize:

A weekend for four (two nights) with Canadian Pacific Hotels and $500 CDN toward the cost of transportation or for use as spending money. See reverse for contest details and rules.

and

Second, Third, and Fourth Prizes:

A set of 16 books by Eric Wilson.

It's easy to enter! Here's all you have to do:

Complete an entry form and name your favourite book by Eric Wilson.

HarperCollins*PublishersLtd*

thanks

CANADIAN PACIFIC

HOTELS

and our media sponsor

putting the cool in school

kidsworld

for their generous support.

Entry form

Print your name, address, and telephone number below and **mail** to the Eric Wilson Million-Copy Man Contest, c/o HarperCollins Publishers Ltd, 55 Avenue Rd., Suite 2900, Toronto, Ontario M5R 3L2

Name:_____

Address:_____

_____Phone:_____

Name your favourite Eric Wilson book:

_____

CONTEST RULES

1. No purchase is required. To enter, print your name, address, and telephone number and name your favourite Eric Wilson book on the contest entry form in this book, or on a plain piece of paper. Limit one entry per individual. All individuals who are students in grades up to and including grade 9 and who are Canadian residents, excluding those who live in Quebec, are eligible to enter, except employees, representatives, and agents of the Sponsor, contest judges, and persons domiciled with any of the above.

2. One grand prize of two nights' accommodation for a maximum of four people at winner's choice of one of the following Canadian Pacific Hotels—Hotel Vancouver or Waterfront Centre Hotel, Vancouver; Jasper Park Lodge, Jasper; Hotel Macdonald, Edmonton; The Palliser or Calgary Airport Hotel, Calgary; Royal York or SkyDome Hotel, Toronto; Château Laurier, Ottawa; The Queen Elizabeth, Montreal; Le Château Frontenac, Quebec City; Hôtel Beauséjour, Moncton; or Hotel Halifax, Halifax—having a value of approximately $800, plus a contribution of $500 CDN toward travel expenses or for use as spending money (for a total approximate value of $1300), will be awarded to the first person whose entry is drawn and who answers a time-limited, mathematical skill-testing question correctly and who complies with the Contest Rules. The grand prize must be taken with an individual over the age of 21 who accepts responsibility for any minors participating in the grand prize. The grand prize includes two nights' accommodation for up to four people—maximum two rooms per night. Food, beverage, travel costs, insurance, and incidental charges are not included and are the winner's responsibility. The winner may take advantage of this prize mid-week or weekend. The stay must be completed by June 1, 1997. Space is subject to availability and blackouts may apply. One set of 16 paperback books by Eric Wilson, having an approximate value of $80, will be awarded to each of the second, third, and fourth person whose entry is drawn and who answers a time-limited, mathematical skill-testing question correctly and who complies with the Contest Rules.

3. Entries must be mailed to the Eric Wilson Million-Copy Man Contest c/o HarperCollins Publishers Ltd, Hazelton Lanes, 55 Avenue Road, Suite 2900, Toronto, Ontario M5R 3L2. **All entries must be received not later than the close of business on December 31st 1996, the Contest Closing Date.** No responsibility will be taken for lost, stolen, misdirected, delayed, destroyed, or illegible entries. All entries become the property of the Sponsor and will not be returned.

4. A random drawing from all entries will be held at 12 noon on January 15th 1997 at the offices of HarperCollins Publishers Ltd, Hazelton Lanes, 55 Avenue Road, Suite 2900, Toronto. Your chance of winning will depend on the number of entries received. The first entry drawn will be for the grand prize. Each of the next three entries drawn will be for a set of 16 paperback books by Eric Wilson.

5. The prizes are not transferable or convertible to cash and must be accepted as awarded. The selected entrant will be contacted by mail and the prizes will be delivered.

6. The selected entrant for any prize and any other person(s) participating in the hotel prize must sign a declaration of compliance with the Contest Rules and a release to obtain the prize. The parent, guardian, or other authorized legal representative of the selected entrant for any prize or other person(s) participating in the hotel prize, if the other person(s) is/are under the age of majority, must also sign a consent and release.

7. The decisions of the contest judges will be final and binding on all entrants. The Sponsor reserves the right to use the winners' or other hotel prize participants' names and/or photographs, without compensation, in any advertising or publicity. This contest is subject to all relevant laws.

8. A copy of the contest rules may be obtained by writing to HarperCollins Publishers Ltd, Hazelton Lanes, 55 Avenue Road, Suite 2900, Toronto, Ontario M5R 3L2.

Not applicable in Quebec.

Have you joined

The *new* Eric Wilson Mystery Club ?

Your membership includes a regular newsletter with lots of exciting contests, prizes, tips on writing, and much more.

If you would like to join the new Eric Wilson Mystery Club, please send a cheque or money order for $12 to the following address:

>Eric Wilson Mystery Club
>Suite 663
>185 - 911 Yates Street
>Victoria, B.C.
>V8V 4Y9

Your annual membership fee will help cover the costs of the club.

DISNEYLAND HOSTAGE

A Liz Austen Mystery

ERIC WILSON

The air was blasted by the huge rotors of a helicopter which roared in above the wall and hovered over the fort, shaking us with the force of the wind storm it created.

On her own during a California holiday, Liz Austen is plunged into the middle of an international plot when a boy named Ramón disappears from his room at the Disneyland Hotel. Has Ramón been taken hostage? Before Liz can answer that question, her own safety is threatened when terrorists strike at the most unlikely target: Disneyland itself.

"When I was reading *Disneyland Hostage* I forgot that a man wrote it. Eric Wilson really knows what girls think."
—*Melissa F., Trail, British Columbia*

THE CASE OF THE GOLDEN BOY

A Tom Austen Mystery

ERIC WILSON

Headlights shone in the distance: a police car, moving fast. It swerved to a stop by the curb, then Officer Larson leapt out and ran swiftly inside. What was going on?

An investigation into the kidnapping of his schoolmate leads young Tom Austen to the seedy Golden Boy Café and an unexpected encounter with a desperate criminal. After getting one step too close to the kidnappers, Tom is taken prisoner and needs all his wits to survive.

The adventures of Tom and Liz Austen are followed by fans of all ages across Canada and abroad in countries like Spain and Japan. Voted 1992 Author of the Year by the Canadian Booksellers Association "for introducing children to the different regions of Canada," Eric Wilson has shown many young people the delights of reading.

"It was fantastic, wonderful, breathtaking, stupendous, amazing and very, very hard to put down. I liked it so much I skipped breakfast to finish it off."

— *Seth R., Massey, Ontario*